D0438857

# More Critical Praise for Achy Obejas

## for *Ruins*

• Selected for the Barnes & Noble Discover Great New Writers program

"In the Havana of *Ruins*, scarcity can only be fought with ingenuity, and the characters work very hard at the exquisite art of getting by. The plot rests on the schemes of its weary, obsessive, dreamy hero—a character so brilliantly drawn that he can't be dismissed or forgotten. A tender and wildly accurate portrait, in a gem of a novel."

—Joan Silber, author of *Fools*

"Usnavy, a man of tender resolve who wants only to do his part as a good revolutionary . . . is nimbly drawn, with genuine depth . . . endearing, sad and funny." —*New York Times Book Review*

"Obejas evinces a new, focused lyricism as she penetrates to the very heart of the Cuban paradox in a story as pared down and intense as its narrator's life." —*Booklist* (starred review)

"[C]ompassionate and intriguing . . . Obejas plays out [the book's] conflicts in measured, simple prose, allowing her descriptions of the mundane— houses, food, dominoes—to illuminate a setting filled with heartbreak, confusion, and decay . . . At her best, Obejas controls the mixture of humor and pathos that suffuse this poor community." —*Los Angeles Times*

"*Ruins* is a beautifully written novel, a moving testament to the human spirit of an unlikely hero who remains unbroken even as the world collapses around him . . . A fine literary achievement, it's Achy Obejas at her very best." —*El Paso Times*

"[A] superb novel." —*Library Journal*

"With the deft and evocative detail of a poet's, Obejas's prose is as illuminating and honest as her struggling protagonist."—*Publishers Weekly*

**Achy Obejas** is the author of the critically acclaimed novels *Ruins*, *Days of Awe*, and three other books of fiction. She edited and translated (into English) the anthology *Havana Noir*, and has since translated Junot Díaz, Rita Indiana, Wendy Guerra, and many others. In 2014, she was awarded a USA Ford Fellowship for her writing and translation.

# THE TOWER OF THE ANTILLES

## SHORT STORIES BY

## ACHY OBEJAS

This is a work of fiction. All names, characters, places, and incidents are the product of the author's imagination or are used fictitiously. Any resemblance to real events or persons, living or dead, is entirely coincidental.

©2017 Achy Obejas
ISBN: 978-1-61775-539-2
Library of Congress Control Number: 2016953888

Achy Obejas
Twitter: @achylandia
Website: www.achyobejas.com

Akashic Books
Twitter: @AkashicBooks
Facebook: AkashicBooks
E-mail: info@akashicbooks.com
Website: www.akashicbooks.com

*Para Cecilia,*
*contigo*
*aquí, allá, y everywhere*

*Siempre he vivido en Cuba.*

—Heberto Padilla, 1968/Lourdes Casal, 1981

# Table of Contents

# THE COLLECTOR

*For Humberto Sánchez*

## 1.

What is your name?

He looked at his passport. There was no question it was him in the photo, that was his name on the blue paper and on the visa attached unevenly to the page. On the tarmac, steam rose from the airplane waiting to leave the island.

He turned. Behind him, past the shadows and the glass partition, there were others—without passports, without visas—schools of them beyond the moist and blurry pane.

What is your name? the uniformed guard at the checkpoint asked again. The guard's eyes darted between the passport and the man, who was still looking over his shoulder at the shimmering aquarium.

The man opened his mouth and pronounced his name with a questioning lilt.

Look at me, said the guard.

But the man was afraid if he took his eyes off what now resembled the quivering lines of a galvanograph, he'd never find that familiar seascape again.

Look at me, said the guard, and this time he stretched his hand and cupped the man's chin, encouraging him.

He said his name once again, this time with more certainty, but his eyes remained fixed on the watery window. There was a bed of tiny fingers along the lower rim and a charm of eyes above them. Figures fluttered: expanding, pausing, contracting; he could almost feel the bodies moving forward, relaxing, then slowly beginning to spin.

Look at me.

Instead, the man lowered his eyes and the aquarium faded into twilight behind him.

## 2.

Before the island had visitors, the natives traveled easier on water than on land. The shoreline served only to launch and beach the smooth dugout shells of maca trees they shaped into canoes, each identical except in length.

In spite of this, the islanders were terrible, unambitious mariners who rarely lost sight of the banks. They depended on the indented shoreline to create bays and lagoons to keep them close to home. Sometimes they'd wait for turtles to lay their eggs, then rush to the sand and flip them on their backs. They'd steal the eggs and slaughter the mothers, fashioning the carapace into combs and hooks for fishing. They found their best trawling where the depth of the continental shelf didn't exceed more than forty fathoms, where the waters were crystalline and warm and they could see the seabed drop to black.

They used bows and arrows, bottom lining, rodding, spearing, seine nets, and fish pots to catch snapper, grouper, garfish, kingfish, lobster, tuna, and shrimp. They had gourds to bail the canoes, to gather rainwater for drinking, and to store their catch. They crafted nose rings, necklaces, and earrings from fish bones and shells and used fish scales to make their bodies sparkle. They had no calendar, no writing system, and kept track of days by counting on their fingers and toes.

### 3.

The orange nylon wrapped around the man's ankle like seaweed. When he bent to pick it up, he saw there were still crumbs of cork inside. He tossed the torn vest, then pulled in his line to cast again. It was early and the water was cool in the bay, the sky silvery. In an hour or two he'd be able to see the black dot of the island in the distance.

The man straightened the line. He'd made the rod

himself, a three-meter bamboo he'd cut, trimmed, sanded, and hung for nine months. In that time, he'd eaten boiled plantains and stared up at the long vertical cane as if in meditation. When he first took it down, he couldn't wait to put a line on it. He ran outside to his suburban yard and whipped it from side to side, the bamboo sizzling through the air. Now he wielded it as if he were stringing a bridge to heaven. The rod aimed, the line rose to the sky instead of the bay.

The orange nylon floated back toward him in a bunch; he grabbed it. Then he saw a metal water bottle, its mouth open. An upside-down tennis shoe skimming the surface. A box of saltines. The man remembered his flight, how he'd pasted his face to the double panes of the window and lost count of the dark shapes in the water. Now his eyes followed the line of debris: a magazine, a compass, the jagged edges of a torn foam floater, a Manila rope like an albino snake curling on the sandy bottom.

## 4.

The first visitors to the islands emerged from a tropical mist on three caravels, each sporting three lateen sails angled against the wind. Each ship ran nearly thirty meters in length and weighed more than ninety tons, dwarfing the native canoes beside them. The glittery islanders stood uneasily on their tiptoes, trying to see beyond the caravels.

Through grunts and signs, the new arrivals and the natives managed to establish some basic communication.

We've come a long way, said the visitors.

But how did you get here? asked the islanders, the fish scales on their bodies twinkling like tiny mirrors.

We sailed on these big boats, said the visitors.

What boats? We see no boats, responded the natives, still standing on their tiptoes, their canoes trembling on the waters.

## 5.

One day, he stumbled on a tiny boat on the shore. He folded it like paper and took it home, setting it in his backyard. The next day, he returned to the same beach and found another craft, this one a long-sided wooden pentagon with slats across it. He dragged it from the water, tied it to the roof of his car, and took it home, placing it next to the paper boat. The day after, he was passing by when he heard a rhythmic thumping and turned off the road, down a dirt path all the way to the water, where he discovered a barge consisting of two long pontoons and a giant metal barrel hitting the rocks with each wave. He pulled it to the shore, then rented a trailer so he could take it home. This one he positioned in the front yard.

Later that week, he came home with a sloop made of balsa wood that had climbed the shore at high tide. Its skin was smooth as a baby's. Soon other crafts found a home in and around his yard—canoes and kayaks, floats built out of driftwood, hollowed tree trunks, discarded refrigerators made buoyant with inflated tubes, car chassis with water wings. A green truck with propellers. Inner tubes piled one on top of the other, filling his garage and blocking his driveway. There were dinghies and skiffs on the roof, and in the neighbors' yards, on homemade trailers in the streets. He sold his bed and slept on a sail he'd strung up like a hammock in his room.

By the time the new year rolled around, he was working three jobs to house the vessels in storage lockers and playgrounds, church parking lots and abandoned rural tracts, in a grassy yard behind a museum, even an airplane hangar. On Saturdays, he took flying lessons so that, eventually, he could reach them before their desolate landing.

## 6.

He would try to explain. He would come in and sit across from the good citizens. He showed them his check stubs from dishwashing, from dog grooming, told them he got paid in cash to pick tomatoes. He had plans for a tower that would display the crafts and tell their stories. The good citizens had grown used to his pleas. They would listen politely then shake their heads. These are ghost tales, they'd say, phantom rafts. After a while, he'd scrape his chair back, get up, and leave.

## 7.

In an overgrown and flooded marsh, alligators rested in the shadows of boats. Herons and egrets stepped gingerly through brackish water. Now and again, a transom moaned as it came loose and eased into the muck. Sometimes a new raft—usually made from truck tubes and bedsheets—would float up by itself, then slip away.

One day, just before sunset, the man drove up wearing wading boots and carrying a toolbox. He surveyed the collection in the reservoir. Then he took a hammer and drill and, one by one, undid each and every vessel, piling the planks, stacking the tires, making a heap of the lawn-mower motors, folding the fabrics left to right into triangles, like a flag. A short distance away, a plane began its descent, its white tail vanishing into the horizon.

# KIMBERLE

"I have to be stopped," Kimberle said. Her breath blurred her words, transmitting a whooshing sound that made me push the phone away. "Well, okay, maybe not have to—I'd say *should*—but that begs the question of why. I mean, who cares? So maybe what I really mean is I need to be stopped." Her words slid one into the other, like buttery babies bumping, accumulating at the mouth of a slide in the playground. "Are you listening to me?"

I was, I really was. She was asking me to keep her from killing herself. There was no method chosen yet—it could have been slashing her wrists, or lying down on the train tracks outside of town (later she confessed that would never work, that she'd get up at the first tremor on the rail and run for her life, terrified her feet would get tangled on the slats and her death would be classified as a mere accident—as if she were that careless and common), or just blowing her brains out with a polymer pistol—say, a Glock 19—available at Walmart or at half price from the same cretin who sold her cocaine.

"Hellooooo?"

"I hear you, I hear you," I finally said. "Where are you?"

I left my VW Golf at home and took a cab to pick her up from some squalid blues bar, the only pale face in the place. The guy at the door—a black man old enough to have been an adolescent during the civil rights era, but raised with the polite deference of the previous generation—didn't hide his relief when I grabbed my tattooed friend, threw her in her car, and took her home with me.

It was all I could think to do, and it made sense for both of us. Kimberle had been homeless, living out of her car—an antique Toyota Corolla that had had its lights punched out on too many occasions and now traveled unsteadily with huge swathes of duct tape holding up its fender. In all honesty, I was a bit unsteady myself, afflicted with the kind of loneliness that's felt in the gut like a chronic and never fully realized nausea.

Also, it was fall—a particularly gorgeous time in Indiana, with its spray of colors on every tree, but, in our town, one with a peculiar seasonal peril for college-aged girls. It seemed that about this time every year, there would be a disappearance—someone would fail to show at her dorm or study hall. This would be followed by a flowering of flyers on posts and bulletin boards (never trees) featuring a girl with a simple smile and a reward. Because the girl was always white and pointedly ordinary, there would be a strange familiarity about her: everyone was sure they'd seen her at the Commons or the bookstore, waiting for the campus bus or at the Bluebird the previous weekend.

It may seem perverse to say this, but every year we waited for that disappearance, not in shock or horror, or to look for new clues to apprehend the culprit: we waited in anticipation of relief. Once the psycho got his girl, he seemed pacified, so we listened with a little less urgency to the footsteps behind us in the parking lot, worried less when out running at dawn. Spared, we would look guiltily at those flyers, which would be faded and torn by spring, when a farmer readying his cornfield for planting would discover the girl among the papery remains of the previous year's harvest.

When Kimberle moved in with me that November, the annual kill had not yet occurred and I was worried for both of us, her in her car and me in my first-floor one-bedroom, the window open for my cat, Brian Eno, to come and go as she pleased. I had trapped it so it couldn't be opened more than a few inches, but that meant it was never closed all the way, even in the worst of winter.

In my mind, Kimberle and I reeked of prey. We were both boyish girls, pink and sad. She wore straight blond hair and had features angled to throw artful shadows; mine, by contrast, were soft and vaguely tropical, overwhelmed by a carnival of curls. We both seemed to be in weakened states. Her girl-friend had caught her in flagrante delicto and walked out; depression had swallowed her in the aftermath. She couldn't concentrate at her restaurant job, mix-ing up simple orders, barking at the customers, so that it wasn't long before she found herself at the unemployment office (where her insistence on step-ping out to smoke cost her her place in line so many times she finally gave up).

It quickly followed that she went home one rosy dawn and discovered her landlord, aware he had no right to do so but convinced Kimberle (now four months late on her rent) would never get it together to legally contest it, had stacked all her belongings on the sidewalk, where they had been picked over by the students at International House, headquar-ters for all the third world kids on scholarships that barely covered textbooks. All that was left were a few T-shirts from various political marches (mostly black), books from her old and useless major in Marxist theory (one with a note in red tucked between its pages which read, *COMUNISM IS DEAD!* which we marveled at for its misspelling), and, to our surprise, her battered iBook (the screen was cracked though it worked fine).

Me, I'd just broken up with my boyfriend—it was my doing, it just felt like we were going nowhere—but I was past the point of righteousness and heavily into doubt. Not about my decision—that, I never questioned—but about whether I'd ever care enough to understand another human being, whether I'd ever figure out how to stay after the initial flush, whether I'd ever get over my absurd sense of self-sufficiency.

When I brought Kimberle to live with me she hadn't replaced much of anything and we emptied the Toyota in one trip. I gave her my futon to sleep on in the living room, surrendered a drawer in the dresser, pushed my clothes to one side of the closet, and explained my alphabetized CDs, my work hours at a smokehouse one town over (and that we'd never starve for meat), and my books.

Since Kimberle had never visited me after I'd moved out of my parents' house—in truth, we were more acquaintances than friends—I was especially emphatic about the books, prized possessions I'd been collecting since I had first earned a paycheck.

I pointed out the shelf of first editions, among them Richard Wright's *Native Son*, Sapphire's *American Dreams*, Virginia Woolf's *Orlando*, a rare copy of *The Cook and the Carpenter*, and Langston Hughes and Ben Carruthers's limited-edition translation of Nicolas Guillén's *Cuba Libre*, all encased in Saran Wrap. There were also a handful of nineteenth-century travel books on Cuba, fascinating for their racist assumptions, and a few autographed volumes, including novels by Dennis Cooper, Ana María Shua, and Monique Wittig.

"These never leave the shelf, they never get unwrapped," I said. "If you wanna read one of them, tell me and I'll get you a copy."

"Cool," she said in a disinterested whisper, pulling off her boots, long, sleek things that suggested she should be carrying a riding crop.

She leaned back on the futon in exhaustion and put her hands behind her head. There was an elegant and casual muscularity to her tattooed limbs, a pliability I would later come to know under entirely different circumstances.

Kimberle had not been installed in my apartment more than a day or two (crying and sniffling, refusing to eat with the usual determination of the newly heartbroken) when I noticed *Native Son* was gone, leaving a gaping hole on my shelf. I assumed she'd taken it down to read when I had turned my back. I trotted over to the futon and peeked around and under the pillow. The sheets were neatly folded, the blanket too. Had anyone else been in the apartment except us two? No, not a soul, not even Brian Eno, who'd been out hunting. I contemplated my dilemma: how to ask a potential suicide if they're ripping you off.

Sometime the next day—after a restless night of weeping and pillow punching which I could hear in the bedroom, even with the door closed—Kimberle managed to shower and put on a fresh black T, then lumbered into the kitchen. She barely nodded. It seemed that if she'd actually completed the gesture, her head might have been in danger of rolling off.

I suppose I should have been worried, given the threat of suicide so boldly announced, about Kimberle's whereabouts when she wasn't home, or what she was up to when I wasn't at my apartment. But I wasn't, I wasn't worried at all. I didn't throw out my razors, I didn't hide the belts, I didn't turn off the pilot in the oven. It's not that I didn't think she was at risk, because I did, I absolutely did. It's just that when she told me she needed to be stopped, I took it to mean she needed me to shelter her until she recovered, which I assumed would be soon. I thought, in fact, I'd pretty much done my duty as a friend by bringing her home and feeding her a cherry-smoked ham sandwich.

Truth is, I was much more focused on the maniac whose quarry was still bounding out there in the wilderness. I would pull out the local print-only paper every day when I got to the smokehouse and make for the police blotter. I knew, of course, that once the villain committed to the deed, it'd be front-page news, but I held out hope for clues from anticipatory crimes.

Once, there was an incident on a hiking trail—two girls were approached by a white man in his fifties, sallow and scurvied, who tried to grab one of them. The other girl turned out to be a member of the campus tae kwon do team and rapid-kicked his face before he somehow managed to get away. For several days after that, I was on the lookout for any man in his fifties who might come in to the smokehouse looking like tenderized meat. And I avoided all trails, even the carefully landscaped routes between campus buildings.

Because the smokehouse was isolated in order to realize its function, and its clientele fairly specialized— we sold gourmet meat (including bison, ostrich, and alligator) mostly by phone and online, though our best seller was summer sausage, as common in central Indiana as Oscar Mayer—there wasn't much foot traffic in and out of the store and I actually spent a great deal of time alone. After I'd processed the orders, packed the UPS boxes, replenished and rearranged the display cases, made coffee, and added some chips to the smoker, there wasn't much for me to do but sit there, trying to study while avoiding giving too much importance to the noises outside that suggested furtive steps in the yard, or shadows that looked like bodies bent to hide below the windowsill, just waiting for me to lift the frame and expose my neck for strangulation.

One evening, I came home to find Kimberle with my Santoku knife in hand, little pyramids of chopped onions, green pepper, and slimy octopus arms with their puckering cups arranged on the counter. Brian Eno reached up from the floor, her calico belly and paws extended toward the heaven promised above.

"Dinner," Kimberle announced as soon as I stepped in, lighting a flame under the wok.

I kicked off my boots, stripped my scarf from around my neck, and let my coat slide from my body, all along yakking about the psychopath and his apparent disinterest this year.

"Maybe he finally died," offered Kimberle.

"Yeah, that's what I thought when we were about fifteen, 'cause it took until January that year, remember? But then I realized it's gotta be more than one guy."

"You think he's got accomplices?" Kimberle asked, a tendril of smoke rising from the wok.

"Or copycats," I said. "I'm into the copycat theory."

That's about when I noticed Sapphire angling in an unfamiliar fashion on the bookshelf. Woolf's *Orlando* was no longer beside it. Had I considered what my reaction would have been any other time, I might have said rage. But seeing the jaunty leaning that suddenly gave the shelves a deliberately decorated look, I felt like I'd been hit in the stomach. I was still catching my breath when I turned around. The Santoku had left Kimberle's right hand, embedding its blade upright on the knuckles of her left. Blood seeped sparingly from between her fingers but collected quickly around the octopus pile, which now looked wounded and alive.

I took Kimberle to the county hospital, where they stitched the flaps of skin back together. Her hand, now bright and swollen like an aposematic amphibian, rested on the dashboard all the way home. We drove back in silence, her eyes closed, head inclined and threatening to hit the windshield.

In the kitchen, the onion and green pepper pyramids were intact on the counter but the octopus had vanished. Smudged paw tracks led out Brian Eno's usual route through the living room window. Kimberle stood unsteadily under the light, her face shadowed. I sat down on the futon.

"What happened to *Native Son* and *Orlando*?" I asked.

She shrugged.

"Did you take them?"

She spun slowly on the heel of her boot, dragging her other foot around in a circle.

"Kimberle . . ."

"I hurt," she said, "I really hurt." Her skin was a bluish red as she threw herself on my lap and bawled.

A week later, *Native Son* and *Orlando* were still missing but Kimberle and I hadn't been able to talk about it. Our schedules failed to coincide and my mother, widowed and alone on the other side of town (confused but tolerant of my decision to live away from her), had gone to visit relatives in Miami, leaving me to deal with her cat, Brian Eno's brother, a daring aerialist she'd named Alfredo Codona, after the Mexican trapeze artist who'd killed himself and his ex-wife. This complicated my life a bit more than usual, and I found myself drained after dealing with the temporarily housebound Alfredo, whose pent-up frustrations tended to result in toppled chairs, broken picture frames, and a scattering of magazines and knickknacks. It felt like I had to piece my mother's place back together every single night she was gone.

One time, I was so tired when I got home I headed straight for the tub and finished undressing as the hot water nipped at my knees. I adjusted the temperature, then I let myself go under, blowing my breath out in fat, noisy bubbles. I came back up and didn't bother to lift my lids. I used my toes to turn off the faucet, then went into a semisomnambulist state in which neither my mother nor Alfredo Codona could engage me, *Native Son* and *Orlando* were back where they belonged, and Kimberle . . . Kimberle was . . . *laughing*.

"What . . . ?"

I sat up, water splashing on the floor and on my clothes. I heard the refrigerator pop open, then tenebrous voices. I pulled the plug and gathered a towel around me, but when I opened the door, I was startled by the blurry blackness of the living room. I heard rustling from the futon, conspiratorial giggling, and Brian Eno's anxious meowing outside the unexpectedly closed window. To my amazement, Kimberle had brought somebody home. I didn't especially like the idea of her having sex in my living room, but we hadn't talked about it—I'd assumed, since she was supposedly suicidal, that there wasn't a need for that talk. Now I was trapped, naked and wet, watching Kimberle hovering above her lover, as agile as the real Alfredo Codona on the high wire.

Outside, Brian Eno wailed, tapping her paws on the glass. I shrugged, as if she could understand, but all she did was unleash a high-pitched scream. It was raining outside. I held tight to the towel and started across the room as quietly as I could. But as I tried to open the window, I felt a hand on my ankle. Its warmth rose up my leg, infused my gut, and became a knot in my throat. I looked down and saw Kimberle's arm, its jagged tattoos pulsing. Rather than jerk away, I bent to undo her fingers, only to find myself face to face with her. Her lips were glistening, and below her chin was a milky slope with a puckered nipple . . . She moved to make room for me as if it were the most natural thing in the world. I don't know how or why but my mouth opened to the stranger's breast, tasting her and the vague tobacco of Kimberle's spit.

Afterward, as Kimberle and I sprawled on either side of the girl, I recognized her as a clerk from a bookstore in town. She seemed dazed and pleased, her shoulder up against Kimberle as she stroked my belly. I realized that for the last hour or so, as engaged as we'd been in this most intimate of maneuvers, Kimberle and I had not kissed or otherwise touched. We had worked side by side—structureless and free.

"Here, banana boat queen," Kimberle said with a sly grin as she passed me a joint. *Banana boat queen? And I thought: Where the fuck did she get that? How the hell did she think she'd earned dispensation for that?*

The girl between us bristled.

Then Kimberle laughed. "Don't worry," she said to our guest, "I can do that; she and I go way back."

In all honesty, I don't know when I met Kimberle. It seemed she had always been there, from the very day we arrived from Cuba. Hers was a mysterious and solitary world. I realized that one winter day in my junior year in high school as I was walking home from school just as dusk was settling in. Kimberle pulled up in her Toyota next to me and asked if I wanted a ride. As soon as I got in, she offered me a cigarette. I said no.

"A disgusting habit anyway. You wanna see something?"

"What?"

Without another word, Kimberle aimed the Toyota out of town, past the last deadbeat bar, the strip malls, and the trailer parks, past the ramp to the interstate, until she entered a narrow gravel road with dry cornstalks blossoming on either side. There was a brackish smell, the tang of wet dirt and nicotine. The Toyota danced on the gravel but Kimberle, bent over the wheel, maintained a determined expression.

"Are you ready?"

"Ready . . . ? For what?" I asked, my fingers clutching the shoulder belt.

"This," she whispered. Then she turned off the headlights.

Before I had a chance to adjust to the tracers, she gunned the car, hurling it down the black tunnel, the tires spitting rocks as she skidded this way and that, following the eerie spotlight provided by the moon . . . For a moment, we were suspended in air and time. My life did not pass in front of my eyes how I might have expected; instead, I saw images of desperate people on a bounding sea; multitudes wandering Fifth Avenue or the Thames, the shores of the Bosporus or the sands outside the pyramids; mirrors and mirrors, mercury and water; a family portrait in Havana from years before; my mother with her tangled hair, my father tilting his hat in New Orleans or Galveston; the shadows of birds of paradise against a stucco wall; a shallow and watery grave, and another longer passage, a trail of bones. Just then the silver etched the sharp edges of the cornstalks, teasing them to life as specters in black coats . . .

"We're going to die!" I screamed.

Moments later, the Toyota came to a shaky stop as we both gasped for breath. A cloud of smoke surrounded us, reeking of fermentation and gasoline. I popped open the door and crawled outside, where I promptly threw up.

Kimberle scrambled over the seat and out, practically on top of me. Her arms held me steady. "You okay?" she asked, panting.

"That was amazing," I said, my heart still racing, "just amazing."

Not even a week had gone by when Kimberle brought another girl home, this time an Eastern European professor who'd been implicated with a Cuban during a semester abroad in Bucharest. Rather than wait for me to stumble onto them, they had marched right into my bedroom, naked as newborns. I was going to protest but was too unnerved by their boldness, and then, in my weakness, I was seduced by the silky warmth of skin on either side of me. Seconds later, I felt something hard and cold against my belly and looked down to see Kimberle wearing a harness with a summer sausage dangling from it. The professor sighed as I guided the meat. While she licked and bit at my chin, Kimberle pushed inch by inch into her. At one point, Kimberle was balanced above me, her mouth grazing mine, but we just stared past each other.

Afterward—the professor between us—we luxuriated, the room redolent of garlic, pepper, and sweat. "Quite the little Cuban sandwich we've got here," Kimberle said, passing me what now seemed like the obligatory after-sex joint followed by a vaguely racist comment. The professor stiffened. Like the bookstore girl, she'd turned her back to Kimberle. Instead of rubbing my belly, this one settled her head on my shoulder, then fell happily asleep.

"Kimberle, you've gotta stop," I said, then hesitated. "I've gotta get my books back. Do you understand me?"

Her head was buried under the pillow on the futon, the early-morning light shiny on her exposed shoulder blade. With the white sheet crumpled halfway up her back, she looked like a headless angel.

"Kimberle, are you listening to me?" There was some imperceptible movement, a twitch. "Would you please . . . I'm talking to you."

She emerged, curtain of yellow hair, eyes smoky. "What makes you think I took them?"

"What? Are you kidding me?"

"Coulda been the bookstore girl, or the professor."

Since the ménage, the bookstore girl had called

to invite me to dinner but I had declined. And the professor had stopped by twice, once with a first edition of Upton Sinclair's *Mental Radio*. Tempting— achingly tempting—as that 1930 oddity was, I had refused it.

"I'll let Kimberle know you stopped by," I'd added, biting my lip.

"I didn't come to see Kimberle," the professor had said, her fingers pulling on my curls, which I'd found disconcerting.

Kimberle was looking at me now, waiting for an answer. "My books were missing before the book-store girl and the professor," I replied.

"Oh."

"We've got to talk about that too."

Down went her head. "Now?" she asked, her voice distant and flimsy like a final communication from a sinking ship.

"Now."

She hopped up, her hip bones pure cartilage. She shivered. "I'll be right back," she said, heading for the bathroom. I dropped back onto the futon, heard her pee into the bowl, then the water running. I scanned the shelf, imagining where *Mental Radio* might have fit. Silence.

Then: "Kimberle? . . . Kimberle, you all right?" I scrambled to the bathroom, struggled with the knob. "Kimberle, please, let me in." I imagined her hanging from the light fixture, her veins cascading red into the tub, that polymer pistol bought just for this moment, when she'd stick its tip in her mouth and . . . "Kimberle, goddamnit . . ." Then I kicked, kicked, and kicked again, until the lock bent and the door gave. "Kimberle . . ." But there was nothing, just my breath misting as I stared at the open window, the screen leaning against the tub.

I ran out and around our building but there was no sign of her, no imprint I could find in the snow, nothing. When I tried to start my car to look for her, the engine sputtered and died. I grabbed the keys to Kimberle's Toyota, which came to life mockingly, and put it into reverse, only to have to brake immediately to avoid a passing station wagon. The Toyota jerked, the duct-taped fender shifted, practically falling, while I white-knuckled the wheel and felt my heart like a reciprocating engine in my chest.

After that, I made sure we spent as much time together as possible: reading, running, cooking venison I brought from the smokehouse, stuffing it with currants, pecans, and pears, or making smoked bison burgers with Vidalia onions and thyme. On any given night, she'd bring home a different girl to whom we'd minister with increasing aerial expertise. At some point I noticed *American Dreams* was missing from the shelf but I no longer cared.

One night in late January—our local psychopath still loose, still victimless—I came home from the smokehouse emanating a mesquite and found a naked Kimberle eagerly waiting for me.

"A surprise, a surprise tonight," she said, helping me with my coat. "Oh my god, you smell . . . *sooooo* good."

She led me to my room, where a clearly anxious, very pregnant woman was sitting up in my bed.

"Whoa, Kimberle, I—"

"Hi," the woman said hoarsely; she was obviously terrified. She was holding the sheet to her ample breasts. I could see giant areolas through the threads, the giant slope of her belly.

"This'll be great, I promise," Kimberle whispered, pushing me toward the bed as she tugged on my sweater.

"I dunno . . . I . . . ."

Before long Kimberle was driving my hand inside the woman, who barely moved as she begged us to kiss, to please kiss for her.

"I need, I need to see that . . ."

I turned to Kimberle but she was intent on the task at hand. Inside the pregnant woman, my fingers took the measure of what felt like a fetal skull, baby teeth, a rope of blood. Suddenly, the pregnant woman began to sob and I pulled out, flustered and confused. I grabbed my clothes off the floor and started out of the room when I felt something soft and squishy under my bare foot. I bent down to discover a half-eaten field mouse, a bloody offering from Brian Eno who batted it at me, her fangs exposed and feral.

I left the dead mouse and apartment behind and climbed into my VW. After cranking it awhile, I managed to get it started. I steered out of town, past the strip malls, the cornfields, and the interstate where, years before, Kimberle had made me feel so fucking alive. When I got to the smokehouse, I scaled up a backroom bunk my boss used when he stayed to smoke delicate meats overnight—it was infused with a smell of acrid flesh and maleness. Outside, I could hear branches breaking, footsteps, an owl. I refused to consider the shadows on the curtainless window. The blanket scratched my skin, the walls whined. Trembling there in the dark, I realized I wanted to kiss Kimberle—not for anyone else's pleasure but for my own.

The next morning, there was an ice storm and my car once more refused to start. I called Kimberle and asked her to pick me up at the smokehouse. When the Toyota pulled up, I jumped in before Kimberle had the chance to park. I leaned toward her but she turned away.

"I'm sorry about last night, I really am," she said, all skittish, avoiding eye contact.

"Me too." The Toyota's tires spun on the ice for an instant then got traction and heaved onto the road. "What was going on with your friend?"

"I dunno. She went home. I said I'd take her but she just refused."

"Can you blame her?"

"Can I . . . ? Look, it was just fun . . . I dunno why everything got so screwed up."

I put my head against the frosty passenger window. "What would make you think that would be fun?"

"I just thought we could, you know, do something . . . *different*. Don't you wanna just do something different now and again? I mean . . . if there's something you wanted to do, I'd consider it."

As soon as she said it, I knew. "I wanna do a threesome with a guy."

"With . . . with a *guy*?"

"Why not?"

Kimberle was so taken back, she momentarily lost control. The car slid on the shoulder then skidded back onto the road.

"But . . . wha . . . I mean, what would I do?"

"What do you think?"

"Look, I'm not gonna . . . and he'd want us to . . ." She kept looking from me to the road, each curve back to town now a little slicker, less certain.

I nodded at her, exasperated, as if she were some dumb puppy. "Well, exactly."

"Exactly? But . . ."

"Kimberle, don't you ever think about what we're doing—about *us*?"

"Us? There is no *us*."

She fell on the brake just as we hurled beyond the asphalt but the resistance was catalytic: the car fishtailed as the rear tires hit the road again. My life such as it was—my widowed mother, my useless Cuban passport, the smoke in my lungs, the ache in my chest that seemed impossible to contain—burned through me. We flipped twice and landed in a labyrinth of pointy cornstalks peppered by a sooty snow. There was a moment of silence, a stillness, then the tape ripped and the Toyota's front end collapsed, shaking us one more time.

"Are you . . . are you okay . . . ?" I asked breathlessly. I was hanging upside down.

The car was on its back, and suddenly *Native Son*, *Orlando*, and *American Dreams* slipped from under the seats, which were now above our heads, and tumbled to the ceiling below us. They were in Saran

Wrap, encased like monarch chrysalides.

"Oh god . . . Kimberle . . ." I started to weep.

She shook her head, sprinkling a bloody constellation on the windshield. I reached over and undid her seat belt, which caused her body to drop with a thud. She tried to help me with mine but it was stuck.

"Let me crawl out and come around," she said, her mouth a mess of red. Her fingers felt around for teeth, for pieces of tongue.

I watched as she kicked out the glass on her window, picked each shard from the frame, and slowly pulled herself through. My head throbbed and I closed my eyes. I could hear the crunch of Kimberle's steps on the snow, the exertion in her breathing. I heard her gasp and choke and then a rustling by my window.

"Don't look," she said, her voice cracking as she reached in to cover my eyes with her ensanguined hands. "Don't look."

But it was too late: there, above her shoulder, was this year's seasonal kill, waxy and white but for the purple areolas and the meat of her sex. She was ordinary, familiar, and the glass of her eyes captured a portrait of Kimberle and me.

*Translated from the original Spanish by the author.*

# ℰXILE

He will get down on his knees.

He will bend his legs and approach us face to face on the deck of the ship. For a moment, it might look like he's going to squat but he doesn't, he just kneels like a penitent, leans back a little, then catches himself and straightens up again. Like davening, but not quite.

This is the myth we tell: about our father as a younger man, kneeling on the deck of a ship, whispering to us about civic society, about Lincoln and the First Amendment.

Actually, that's not true. He would never have talked about the First Amendment. He would have more likely mentioned democracy—or freedom. That's the word he liked the most.

We keep this secret: The iron hissing on the dining room table, the towels moist, our mother's hair splayed on the cloth, her chin just off the edge. A black thread of smoke.

And this one: the champagne bottle a brutal club

in her hand, the champagne an arch like a morning star.

But not these: The bar on US 12 with sawdust on the floor. The bar at the mall that stayed open past the shopping center's closing hours. The bar downtown where the high school teachers held their book club discussions and gossiped and flirted and gave each other strategic rides home that were acted out as spontaneous.

We wanted to be Jews.

We wanted to be Polish or German. We would have settled for Danish.

A boy with relatives in Copenhagen explained to us that all blue-eyed people on earth are related to a single ancestor whose genes mutated between six and ten thousand years ago.

We explained that where we come from the greatest achievement is to leave.

Most of us held clerical, semiskilled, and service jobs, our median income well below the national norm. We preferred to think we were lawyers, doctors, teachers, paramedics, industry giants, the president of Coca-Cola, unbelievably popular and successful pop stars, and media titans. We cared for our grandparents, our cousins, our aunts and uncles, for the offspring of the friends who didn't make it over, for our own kids when they refused to leave home. We had nuclear households plus one, sometimes two.

We curled into a ball, all of us, in the backseat of that Pontiac. We did not want to look, to hear the altercation outside, by the gas pump. We prayed no one would notice us, our pink flesh, our red lips; we prayed no one would ask for the words we could not form with our stiff fingers, force like a cough from our bruised mouths.

When a cousin refused breakfast—a fried egg, a slab of grilled ham, and greasy toast—we witnessed an uncle push her chair closer to the table. She was wearing flannel and had a rash. Hours later, he piled lunch next to the fried egg, ham, and toast: a hill of rice, a smear of spicy ground beef. She swung her legs, meaty little limbs tolling away the hours. In late afternoon, a glass of milk, a banana. For dinner came a cut of liver, onions browned in its juice, a bowl of Neapolitan ice cream with three bulging scoops.

He was making a point.

We listen, enraptured, to the moon landing on a radio in Loomis Park in Miami Beach. We are aware there are 227 kinds of birds in the Grand Canyon, only twenty-six fish. We admire public art. We are citizens and we vote, not for a particular party, but for, and against, ideas. We know the Gettysburg Address and its admonitions to us, the living.

A man named Walter Poenisch once made the same trip we did, only he swam it. He rotated his body along its long axis with every arm stroke, so that the shoulder of the recovering arm was always higher than the shoulder of the other arm, the one that pushed and pulled.

This way, there will always be less need to turn to breathe. When one shoulder is out of the water, it reduces drag; when it falls, it aids the arm catching the water; when the other shoulder rises, it will help the arm at the other end of the push to leave the water.

When we heard about the trip, at first we thought Walter Poenisch had done it in reverse, from here to there. Then we read that it wasn't ninety miles but 129, that he took necessary breaks for medical purposes, and that it took him thirty-four hours, protected in a shark cage.

# The Sound Catalog

*The radiator hissing.*

Dulce considered the radiator's thin, moist emission, the mist like when ironing a linen shirt. She turned over on the bed, burying her good ear between her head and the pillow. She liked the feel of the sheets, clean and crisp. She liked the sound of that radiator, even when it was muffled and what she was really listening to was the memory of it. She'd never seen such a thing in Cuba, never heard its song, never touched it before. Her hand had been drawn to it when she and her Cuban ex-lover moved into their first apartment, their fourth day in the US, their third in Chicago. Even now, she could still hear her flesh sizzle. She felt the memory of that too, when she reached over to her night table for the little box. She flipped it open, plucked out a creamy pink hearing aid, and poked it in her right ear, then the other in her left. Each time, her fingertips pulsed as the aids trilled awake.

*The mob shouting as one, the crowd rallied to a frenzy.*

This is the story they told, she and her Cuban ex-lover, about their lives back on the island: That they were hiding from the neighbors, the windows shuttered, lights off. They had decided to skip the rally, to avoid the marathon at the plaza. Her Cuban ex-lover's father sat in a rocking chair, listening to a banned radio station through earphones. Her Cuban ex-lover's mother sat in her own rocker across from him, reading a detective novel with a pocket flashlight. Dulce remembered the chairs squeaking, the occasional static and the crackling of pages. And she and her Cuban ex-lover—a sweet, round girl she'd known and loved forever—in the bedroom across from them, the door closed and latched. She had a distinct memory of the click, of the wooden door groaning when she tugged at it.

This was all routine: the father with his radio, the mother reading by clandestine light, the door resisting. It had all happened before: the silent kisses, the silent unzipping, the silent lowering of her mouth, the silent touch of tongue on belly and tongue on thigh and tongue on clit. Dulce was so burrowed in silence, so deep in the sea, that she could feel tissues dissolving, nerves misfiring. The room spun and she laughed, and then the room spun a bit more and her tongue lost its place and she looked up and her Cuban ex-lover, sitting spread-eagled and wide-eyed, poked Dulce's shoulder so she'd turn around. And there, at the threshold of the door, her Cuban ex-lover's father, eyes lowered to something he was brushing from his shirt, closed the bedroom doors blown open, while behind him the wind bellowed through the open window in the living room and her Cuban ex-lover's mother struggled with the shutters. Dulce had missed the thunder that drove the thousands from the plaza, the window clattering open, the boom of the bedroom door exploding into tongue on clit and belly and thigh; she hadn't heard the scrambling of feet, the rocker falling over, the flashlight tumbling to the ground and cracking its glass eye.

They gathered themselves and walked out of the bedroom as if there had been no storm, and nodded and stared at the broken flashlight and then talked in low tones about spare parts and answered in girlish voices her Cuban ex-lover's father's invitation to rice pudding in the kitchen.

*The teapot whistling, not much differently than the radiator hissing.*

Dulce had given up coffee, because of the caffeine. She'd thought it would be difficult after a lifetime of coffee: café con leche every morning of her life, the leche part not always real but the coffee, for the most part, had been real enough. Back in Cuba, sometimes her mother or her Cuban ex-lover would crush peas to stretch the coffee to fill the coffeemaker that would hiss like the radiator she didn't know yet and not so much like the teapot she'd since adopted in its stead. Café con leche and peas.

Later it turned out the best part of the café con leche was the peas. The peas had fiber, so much Vitamin A and C, while the coffee upped stress, digestive discomfort, and constriction of the blood vessels in her inner ears. Dulce drank herbal teas now, blends her non-Cuban lover had devised—caffeine-free and surprisingly flavorful. Sometimes there'd be homemade chai (It's a different kind of caffeine, her non-Cuban lover had said), and sometimes, too, there'd be dinner recipes with peas that never failed to surprise her: pea and mint pesto, buttered peas and wilted lettuce, peas deglazed in white wine, herbed pea soup, sweetbreads with pea foam. She didn't miss the coffee, she didn't miss the gravelly sound of the grinder forcing the peas and coffee beans together. She swatted the memory of her café con leche away.

Dulce stirred and sipped her tea and padded into her beauty shop. She loved that she could hear the soft squeak of her snow boots on the linoleum accompanied by a slight electronic echo in her ears. It was snowing outside, which meant she was wearing layers of scarves that would brush her ears during the day, the noise like hurricane winds.

*The drone of the television in the background.*

In Cuba, the TV was always on somewhere; indeed, two or three or four TVs would layer the sound of the one or two legal channels over the one or two or three illegal channels inevitably playing in her neighbors' houses. The soundtracks would duel in the courtyard and on the street, compete with the growling of old auto engines and the banter coming from the same neighbors whose TVs were on, ignored, their volume a comfort rather than a necessity. They all half heard and half read lips and eyebrows, the angle of shoulders, and the ways fingers pointed in the air.

Her Cuban ex-lover was part of the symphony and the drama. Her voice had a high pitch, an ascension nearly into falsetto. And Dulce had loved and hated it—hated the sound, considered it tasteless and extravagant, but loved that she knew what it meant: unbearable excitement, for good or bad. Her Cuban ex-lover's hands fluttered like a bird flying against the wind.

The last years they lived in Cuba, her Cuban ex-lover was always up in those high registers: be-

cause there were no limes in all of Havana, because
a man had groped her on the bus, because a friend
got a visa and now there was a farewell party, because that same friend's absence meant she'd get a
promotion at work that would bring more responsibility than she wanted, because a French bakery they
couldn't afford had opened off La Rampa, because
can you believe it, Dulcita, Wanda has joined the
Ladies in White and is going all over the city with
those people.

Dulce had seen them, of course: the women pa-
rading in silence, protesting the imprisonment of
their men—husbands and sons and brothers and
partners. In those years, the women weren't beaten
and dragged into buses. Instead, the authorities simply pretended they didn't exist, which extended
permission to everyone else to do the same. Dulce
and her Cuban ex-lover would turn their heads as
the women came up their street, focus on the TV visible through someone's open door, and pretend to
lose themselves in whatever soap opera was airing.
No one would make eye contact or talk—it was as if
life was a silent film that had slipped into slow motion and only returned to its normal pace when the
women had passed.

It was later that her Cuban ex-lover began to
look up, to nod at the women. And later still when

that nod transformed from the barely perceptible to the very pronounced. At night, Dulce would turn up the volume of their own TV so the neighbors and the mics embedded in the walls wouldn't pick up and then she'd whisper, What are you doing? Are you crazy?

Because Dulce didn't want any trouble: Her father and older brother had long ago rowed an inner tube to Miami and claimed both her and her mother via family reunification, but in their first five years in the US her father and brother (who'd become a meth addict, unbeknownst to her then) had only been able to save enough to get her mother out of Cuba and to Chicago (where her brother was in treatment, also unbeknownst to her then). She didn't want anything to be used as an excuse to keep her from going when the time came and that plane ticket and visa were in hand.

I don't want any trouble, Dulce would say, and the air would fill with all she couldn't say: the confusion and guilt she felt since she hadn't seen her father and brother in a decade and could barely remember them, because in the five years since her mother had gone she'd practically been adopted by her Cuban ex-lover's family, yet she still felt an overwhelming obligation to go, no matter how happy she and her and her ex-lover were, hiding in her room on

Sundays, later living together, setting up their own home in her family's old apartment. I don't want any trouble, Dulce would whisper into the noise meant to render the eavesdropping futile. But she would not say, I don't want to talk about having to leave, about my chances of leaving, about all I will miss if I leave, just as much as I don't want to talk about staying . . .

And her Cuban ex-lover—who may or may not have heard her through the cheering on the TV screen celebrating socialism's rebirth in Hugo Chávez—winked at her as she passed by in a hush, dressed in a blinding white that left Dulce and her neighbors with their mouths agape.

*A bell.*

The ESL instructor tried to liven up the class by bringing in props to illustrate American expressions. One day it was a bell. Whenever you hear a bell ring, she said, anger turns on a swing. It made no sense to Dulce but she repeated it anyway: Anger turns on a swing.

Maybe, said her Cuban ex-lover when she told her about it at home, your teacher means that when the bell goes off, like in a boxing match, anger fuels the boxer's punch, his swing.

Dulce was always impressed with her Cuban

ex-lover's efforts to make sense of the nonsensical. Except this still didn't seem quite right: there was a tenderness that accompanied the instructor's telling that didn't go with the brutality of a boxer's angry wallop. She wished her Cuban ex-lover was going to ESL classes with her, but she had refused. (Dulce would have asked her father or mother or brother to go, but their English was already too advanced for ESL classes.)

It's boring! her Cuban ex-lover would exclaim, her voice up in the stratosphere, her hands a blur. I'm either going to learn English or I'm not, but I'm not going to waste hours of my life sitting there listening to crazy lines I'm never going to use like, *Whenever you hear a bell ring, anger turns on a swing.* When will I ever need to say that, huh?

Years later, it occurred to Dulce she'd never heard anyone say it either. She turned to her non-Cuban lover and asked when it might be appropriate.

Anger turns on a swing? her non-Cuban lover said.

Yes, whenever you hear a bell ring . . .

An angel earns its wings!

What?

That's the saying: *Whenever you hear a bell ring, an angel earns its wings.*

Dulce knew sometimes she missed things—like

the wind that day blasting in her Cuban ex-lover's family's house, or the specials as enumerated by an indifferent waiter—but she attributed it more to her character than to any fault of her ears. She was, by nature or training, someone who'd found it best to not pay too much attention. And now—English wasn't her language.

I hear fine in Spanish, she said, though she wondered if her affirmation didn't sound more like a question.

I think, her non-Cuban lover said, that you compensate. And anyway, you only hear fine in Spanish when you're talking to other Cubans. You don't hear Mexicans or Guatemalans.

They speak so softly.

They move their mouths differently.

It's just that Cubans are disoriented out of Cuba.

*The zzzzzzz of the zippers.*

Dulce figured that was why her Cuban ex-lover was so sour after the first few months off the island: she was disoriented. They'd been caught up in the excitement: the unlikelihood that they'd both gotten visas to the US at the same time, the reconciliation with her parents in Chicago, and the shock of their acceptance of her relationship with her Cuban ex-lover. It's not that her family didn't know—everyone knew, she and her Cuban ex-lover had been stuck on each other since grade school and sometime around sixth grade everyone understood they were a couple—but no one had ever talked about it before, not openly, not to Dulce's face, not in any way she could hear and understand. But in Chicago, her parents told them they would need privacy and thus had rented them their own studio apartment. Her brother, who spoke in a flat voice now, told them about the county's domestic partner registry, which would guarantee them a few rights. He seemed to know a lot about social services and gave them a contact number for a group of Latina lesbians that met once a month.

But after going to a few events—a cold picnic on Lake Michigan where she and her Cuban ex-lover almost froze and a poetry reading neither of them cared for—her Cuban ex-lover declared she was bored by the Latina lesbians. What do I have in common with them? she asked.

Well, I liked the linguistics professor. And the restaurant owner, Dulce said.

I can't understand the restaurant owner. If that's Spanish she's speaking, I'm Jennifer López. And the linguistics professor's Bosnian partner is too post-Soviet for my taste.

Too post-Soviet for your taste?

I just mean we don't have anything in common

with them, her Cuban ex-lover said. They never had to stand in line for food because of a blockade.

Please, those people had bombs raining down on them.

See? I just don't want to have these conversations. I thought we came here to avoid all that.

Dulce zipped up her coat, zipped up her boots and gloves, and stared at her. In a moment, she was surrounded by the cold comfort of snow all around her.

*The announcement over the PA system at the grocery store.*

Dulce thought she was done with Cuban politics when they left the island. She thought being in Chicago, away from Miami's expat intrigue, confirmed it. They could, she thought, pretend they'd never had anything to do with any of it. Because, as much as Dulce missed her girlfriend's family, her neighbors and friends, as much as she longed for the easy rhythm of life in her neighborhood and the sweet gossip and predictability of her work as a receptionist at a local beauty salon, there were many more things she was glad to be rid of: the almost daily shock of finding someone she knew had emigrated, the effort of decoding government language about things as simple as the availability of services at a clinic or gas station, the still-potent power of political proximity to decision-makers. She begrudged no one their good luck in being born to a revolutionary family, but she found it depressing and paralyzing that it was nearly impossible to rise to the same level through study or work. Besides, she liked the frivolity of American life: she liked what seemed like infinite choices for TV watching; she loved that the privacy of her home was, if not absolute, at least fairly convincing; she loved that there were thirty different kinds of soy sauce at the grocery store.

Her Cuban ex-lover, by contrast, hated that there was so little to do (unless you had money) and so much trash on TV, and she found the thirty different kinds of soy sauce overwhelming: I just want normal soy sauce, *normal* soy sauce! she cried at the top of her lungs in the international foods aisle as the PA blared overhead and the store's security guard ran toward them, gun drawn, to find out what was going on.

*A thousand katydids.*

The first day of beauty school, the teacher had all the students design a vision board. Dulce listened intently; she wasn't sure she'd heard right. But by the time that first class period ended, Dulce had constructed the best vision board of all the cosmotology students; naturally, the esthetic students had more complex and colorful boards. The lone guy in the class—an esti, of course—even included a pop-up cruise ship in his. Dulce had watched as he began to construct it, coming close and asking questions until she realized what the assignment was really about. The guy was so pleased with her interest in his that he helped with hers: drawing a sunny and light-filled salon with happy clients getting their hair cut, their nails done, and their pores scrubbed. Meaning that Dulce's vision board was pretty damn good: her own salon, with six chairs for hair, four for mani/pedis, and two for facials. Then the instructor suggested there might be too many resources focused on non-hair client services. Dulce dropped the facials and two of the mani/pedi chairs but only to please the teacher. She knew exactly where she wanted to set up, and who her clientele would be—young Latina professionals and older women like her mother, all anxious and hardworking—so she needed the mani/pedi and facial stations for when they wanted to reward themselves.

Her Cuban ex-lover had not been at all pleased with Dulce's beauty school plans. Twenty thousand dollars in tuition? she asked. She was waiting tables at a restaurant owned by a Cuban friend of Dulce's family and making a boatload on Saturday-night tips (most of which she sent back to her parents in Cuba, and the rest she saved for a ticket to visit as soon as possible, so that she and Dulce were always on a tight budget and Dulce's tuition depended on loans). Why can't you just keep cutting hair at home? That way we don't need to get a license or rent a place.

But Dulce knew, watching the stylists at Paul Mitchell's school through the glass windows downtown, a Starbucks chai in hand, that whatever else leaving Cuba meant, it was a chance for reinvention. And part of that meant no standing on the sidelines. Besides, she was clear she wasn't a great stylist. Her hope rested on being good enough to get licensed and saving enough money to set up a business where she could hire people who cut like those at Paul Mitchell: snips of hair flying around their chairs, scissors clicking like a thousand katydids.

*The Cuban national anthem.*

Having failed to find community with lesbians, Dulce and her Cuban ex-lover began to hang out with other Cubans. In Chicago, this meant small groups, usually populated by people who'd come decades before them and were much better off, but who appreciated their recent arrival as a confirmation of their decision to leave all those years before. Dulce didn't mind their gatherings too much. There was Cuban food, much of it new to her (she'd had plenty of ham sandwiches on the island but she'd never had a Cuban sandwich, per se, until she left Cuba), and old-school Cuban music (not the Buena Vista Social Club, of which she was so tired, but singers who predated many of their new friends' own youth). She didn't recognize the Cuba they longed for but she enjoyed speaking Spanish—her easy, casual Spanish—and loved that everyone told the same jokes over and over.

Her Cuban ex-lover seemed at home too. She got involved with putting together a community directory and quickly learned everyone's names and stories; she helped bring one of the Ladies in White over for a tour of the US and raised funds for the group. Eventually, she got herself elected as secretary of the Cuban American Chamber of Commerce even though she wasn't a business owner, but in anticipation of Dulce's soon-to-open beauty salon. When the time came, some of the old Cuban guys from Goya Foods helped Dulce get a Small Business Administration loan.

At all the formal Cuban events, they played the national anthem: *Morir por la patria es viviiiiiiiiiiir!* A new Cuban friend told them that the man who wrote the lyrics shouted that very line just before he was killed by a firing squad. And it's so true, he said, to die for your country is to live! Her Cuban ex-lover enthusiastically agreed, and the two of them—their new friend and her Cuban ex-lover—talked for a very long time about the meaning of patriotism and martyrdom.

Dulce hadn't heard most of the conversation but when they turned to their own suffering as exiles, she decided to go help clean up in the kitchen. It was tiring to try to keep up, to decipher whole sentences from two or three words. As she was tying a knot on a garbage bag, she felt someone grab her elbow. She turned. C'mon, a woman she'd seen a couple of times before said to her. What's going on? she asked. Can't you hear, there's a fight. When Dulce stepped back in the dining hall, she saw her Cuban ex-lover being held back by the Goya guys who'd cosigned her business loans. Her Cuban ex-lover's chin was out, her screaming as high as a police whistle. Her hands reached out to slap their new friend, who was facing her and holding a fork like a weapon. You fucking communist! he shrieked at her.

*Gunshots.*

The drive home, punctuated by gunshots crackling just off Western and North avenues, was paused when they were forced to pull over to let a fleet of squad cars go by, lights flashing. Dulce barely heard her Cuban ex-lover's explanation: her ears felt full and the lights of the police cars, now blinking white, had given her a headache. But she knew what had happened because it wasn't the first time. The argument had already been rehearsed with her brother, who'd been too anesthetized to push back in any way. The reasons for the two of them coming over were in a process of transformation, and there were no sides to take yet. Dulce had come to her own understanding, but her Cuban ex-lover was still bitterly pushing and pulling, trying to find a rationalization that fit.

You know I'm right, she finally said. And when Dulce didn't respond, concentrating instead on the police barricade, her Cuban ex-lover punched her shoulder. Did you hear me? Are you really deaf or are you just pretending so you don't have to say anything to me? I'm not sure I can live like this, not knowing if you're pretending.

Do you see this? Dulce said, her finger making circles in the air to indicate the police encirclement.

Do you hear me? Do you hear me at all? Do you hear me anymore?

*Breathing.*

Dulce thought a lot about silence, about its formless, odorless existence. She thought of it as an ever-present gas or pollen. At first, it terrified her.

At night or in the early hours of dawn, she would sometimes tap her thigh or shuffle her feet just to check that she could, in fact, still hear. She treasured the popping of fat in the frying pan, the clicking of her tongue. In summer, she tapped the radiator, remembering its hiss during the polar months. In winter, she would zip and unzip her coat, imprinting the soundtrack. She avoided salt and gluten—she couldn't begin to imagine what her Cuban ex-lover would have to say about such a diet—and rattled the cutlery on her plate.

But sometime after her Cuban ex-lover went for her visit to Cuba (from which, it turned out, she would never return), Dulce began to sense the arrival of the bus in her peripheral vision from blocks away. And to feel the footsteps of others in her own soles. When she felt a tingling in her ears, she would tap a clip from her auditory memory and know it was the brass braying in a favorite song.

One winter day at the shop, she turned on the TV and watched the American president with incredulity. Weeks later, she found a video streaming live from the island in which officers from various ministries talked about what lay ahead. Behind them stood several attendants dressed in olive green. Dulce watched a familiar figure scribbling on a clipboard. She sipped her tea and turned off the TV. She didn't need to wait for her to take a turn at the podium to imagine the high-frequency sound of her convictions.

What do you think . . . a client asked as Dulce snipped her hair, but the last words faded into the colorless void.

Dulce went through her sound catalog to fill in the blank, replayed the client's lips moving in the mirror, and tried to decode their meaning. She took a long breath, felt it moving in her lungs and chest, then let it out, savoring its sweet emission.

# North/South

## 1.

Her boot bumped her husband's foot. It had stopped snowing and he was slumbering on his left side by the frozen river. His body formed an S, a downy white S, and only when she pulled her boot back and aimed the flashlight did she see beyond the cover of snow. His hair, wet and sprinkled with flakes, coiled from under the folds of his black wool hat like a flat snake.

Hey, she whispered. She brushed the snow from his face. She pulled off her glove, put her hand on his cool cheek, then pushed her way around his scarf and collar. His neck was cold too, but he was breathing, slow and shallow.

Hey, she said again, this time not a whisper, though out here on the riverbank, with the netting of branches around her, her voice sounded trapped.

His eyes were closed, a shiver on his lids.

She jostled his elbow, sending a miniature snow cliff avalanching down his back. His skin was red where the shirt separated from his pants. This time she would not sit with him, would not rock him back to warmth, would not pray to be found when her cell refused to connect with a satellite.

Come on, she said, smoke in the thin cold air.

She stuck the flashlight in her coat sleeve, pushed it up almost to her elbow so it'd shine, while allowing her hands to be free. Then she pulled her arm up like a crane and directed the light to the river. She spied his coat half buried in the snow on the icy surface. She could hear a thrashing, but she wasn't sure if it was ice breaking or sleeves flapping.

She laid the blanket she'd brought with her on the ground behind her husband, then pushed him on his back. She undid the cuffs of his oversized shirt and pulled them together, tied them in a knot. She tucked his bare hands into his pants, even reached in and yanked the band of his underwear up and around his wrists. She knew she'd have to stop later and repeat it all when his hands slid out, blue and hard, or when the shirtsleeves ripped or came undone.

She pried his legs apart, stepped between them with her back to him, and heaved them up, one in each hand. The first step was the toughest, and the flashlight in her sleeve slipped out and fell into the snow. She watched it sink headfirst as the hot bulb melted the snow. She decided she didn't need the light, turned it off, and tucked it into her coat pocket. Then she picked up her husband's legs again, gripped his ankles right at the boots.

Bird bones, she thought once she took her second and third steps. She leaned into it, four, five, seven, twelve steps.

She had lost count when the song came into her head: *For the first quarter of a mile / He'll only charge a pretty girl a smile / For every quarter after this / He'll collect a kiss / When the moon is high and the ladies sigh / The rickety rickshaw comes a creakin'* . . .

## 2.

The boy lay back on the counter, the wood warm against his already moist and sticky skin, and swatted at the flies insisting on crawling up his nose.

Your nostrils are too big, his sister said, they're like caverns. A fly could make a home there, hang off your boogers like a bat on a stalactite.

He waved his hands, covered the lower half of his face. His eyes, enormous: trembling brown disks surrounded by red lightning. He looked sick, as if he might throw up any minute.

Here, his sister said, handing him a green bandanna, use this. But you might look like a bandit.

He shot up, ripping his skin off the wood. The medal around his neck had slipped and now hung off his back. He adjusted it, swinging it up front, just below the hollow of his clavicles.

*Como el mar espera al río,* the radio sang. *Así espero tu regreso / A la tierra del olvido.*

The phone rang: a squat black thing like a broad-shouldered Buddha with a wreath on its belly. A bulbous green fly alighted where the head might have been. For one split second, they both held their breath. It was the wrong time for their father to call: too early in the day, and the wrong day.

It was his sister who grabbed the receiver, sending the fly wobbling into the humid air. Taffa's Grocery & Messenger Service, she said into the mouthpiece, but before she'd even finished, the clarity on the other end indicated it was a local call. She hadn't yet let her breath out when her brother snatched the phone, almost losing his balance on the counter as he pushed the bandanna into his pocket. There was a swath of red on his back, like a burn.

This is my job, he hissed at her. Then, into the phone: Taffa's Grocery & Messenger Service, how can I help you?

Who is it?

Uh-huh, he said, nodding into the receiver and swatting at the flies orbiting his head. He was tethered to the counter by the chewed-up phone cord. He put the phone down. It's for the Beauty Queen.

But who is it?

I don't know, he said as he turned around, but don't hang up. His feet smacked the wooden slats of the grocery store then hit the dirt. He pumped his arms as he ran past the key chain vendor and Lalo's father's flower cart filled with celestinas and beautiful bayahibe roses, past the post office and the Western Union that everyone called the money store, down the road to the rusted chain-link fence surrounding the Beauty Queen's house. He scaled the fence, already bent and wobbly, rather than try and undo the wiry mess the Beauty Queen used as a latch.

Phone call! Phone call! he screamed, waving his arm for balance on the sloping chain link. It was then, at that precise moment, that the orange metal mesh gave him a boost, and his feet lifted off, first the heel, then the inner and outer arch, then the mounds of his soles, so he felt when his second and third toes grazed the links and his body shot upward, the medal around his neck now even with his mouth, the chain glancing off his cheek like a fat fly.

Phone call! he screamed as gravity towed him down. Phone call! This time, when the balls of his feet hit the mesh, the fence bent, dipped lower, hurling him even higher so he could see beyond the roof of the Beauty Queen's haggard home, right to the green of the ocean—a shallow tropical green—and the medal almost tipped into his mouth, so that, still rising, he could lean his head forward like a hungry baby and pull it to him with his tongue, his knees also rising as if he were climbing an invisible stairway . . . and then down, past the slope to a dip in the mesh, to an absence of fence, to the hard ground: a clatter, a triangle of rusty links jabbing at his belly.

Do not jump on my fence! screamed the Beauty Queen, a blur of color unlatching the fence and running past him, splayed like a starfish. She was a dust storm down the road to Taffa's Grocery & Messenger Service.

He got up tentatively, the fence shaky beneath him. He wiped his face; the back of his hand smeared blood from his mouth—he hadn't realized he'd cut his lip. He brushed the rust from the skin of his tight round belly.

The medal—a Saint Christopher medal—had fallen from the chain. When he went to reach for it, it hurt to bend. He scooped it up, rose slowly, then searched for the broken link. He put the links together, then placed the broken one between his teeth to press it closed. It tasted like dirt.

He walked back to Taffa's, past the money store, the post office, Lalo's father's flower cart, and the key chain vendor. He noticed a man with tiny round glasses setting up by the key chains, sorting a dozen woven palm-leaf wallets on a mat on the ground.

He lay back down on the counter and felt a chill. The radio was off. Her call finished, the Beauty Queen turned to him and unleashed a stream of admonishments about jumping on her fence; it was not the first time. He stared at her, at the thick mascara outlining her eyes in a manner long out of style. A fly the size of a peanut buzzed into his line of vision, obscuring and replacing the Beauty Queen's face.

Are you listening to me? she demanded, and poked him hard in the stomach so the first knuckle of her index finger sank into his flesh. He yelped, sprang up as if the skin on his belly had been pierced.

You hear me? she said, cupping his chin with her other hand. Such melodrama, such an actor, she said, bringing his face millimeters from hers, jutting her chin out at him.

She let him go with a push. He dropped back, breathless now, mouth open and loose, the Saint Christopher medal on his cheek.

### 3.

Her daughter Mari is talking about sewing fireflies, red and green, on her dress. This, Mari says, is what she wants to wear on her birthday. There's a tribe of cousins between the ages of four and twelve collecting them in soda bottles. (It's hard with such a narrow opening.)

It'll be so beautiful! the girl exults.

She listens as her daughter tells her she doesn't need or want a party, though it's already started: uncles sitting on the front porch drinking and arguing while a tempest rolls slowly up the beach; aunts in the kitchen, as if all the food they've spent the last few days preparing is still destined for the festively decorated tables in front of the house, their legs embedded in sand. The water is low here, cut off by a sandbar not too far out.

The rain begins, big heavy drops that pierce the shore break. The sea foam reminds her of snow: the snow they've temporarily fled, the snow they'll return to for reassurance. When the water pulls back and the lather breaks into spidery threads, she thinks of the intricacy of snowflakes, how the twinkling lace thins to vanish.

The night before, there had been dancing and tripping on beach chairs. A local boy played bongos, another strummed a guitar. Her husband put a pair of maracas in her hands and then wrapped them in his and moved them up and down, a stiff shake that produced more of a thud than the usual *ch-ch-che*.

You don't have to be an island girl to know how to do this, he'd said.

Except she is, but from a different island. The one they never have enough money to visit, the one with its own fireflies: *Alecton discoidalis*, yellow, with black tips on the antennae, a yellow border along the wing casings. They flash yellow, not red, a bright and cautionary yellow.

Are you telling me I'm drunk? he'd leaned in to whisper. Is that it? He'd stepped back, his mouth lopsided, and shook the maracas in her grip, this time sliding his hands back so he held only the bulbs with his fingertips. You should try it sometime, he'd said, meaning drunkenness. It releases the pain, he'd added with a sick grin.

This was before the argument with the other vacationers—Americans who he and the uncles had determined were enjoying the island and the island-ers too much, and for all the wrong reasons. We are from here! the uncles had shouted. From here! he'd chorused, though he only came for two or three weeks every year now, and there was a time when he hadn't even come that often—first because he couldn't afford it, and then because he couldn't take it, as there was too much evidence of his previous absences.

We are from here!

She'd had to pull him away, rescue him from the weaving cars on the access road to the beach, and lift him onto a kitchen chair after he'd slipped coming into the cabin. His balance had been off since he'd lost two toes to frostbite months ago. It was a miracle he hadn't upset the pots of food the aunts were preparing: fish marinading in orange and lime juice, sliced red onions pickling in vinegar.

Later, after he'd passed out on a plate smeared with black beans, she and Mari had had to push and shove him into bed. She had been taking his pants off, barely remembering a time when they'd sighed into each other, when he suddenly opened his eyes and said, My pain is greater, it's always greater, it is the greatest pain of all.

Now, as the rain picks up and the ocean swirls, her attention is drawn to the shore. One of the uncles has written a love poem, not necessarily to his wife—he won't say—and has rolled it up, tucked it inside a bottle, and cast it into the stormy sea. When he arches his arm, the bottle shoots out at a short, sharp angle and hits the waves right on the shore.

This is not the uncle who once worked in a steel mill hauling sheets, but the one who owns a beauty shop where Taffa's Grocery & Messenger Service used to be. (No one can believe he has the nerve to rent out that place.)

They both notice, she and her husband, the moment their daughter gives up the hunt for fireflies.

How Mari's head turns, almost robotically, and lasers in on the spot where the uncle's bottle has disappeared in the bubbling waters like a satellite fallen out of orbit.

There's thunder as the girl pivots and sprints. A flash of lightning. The cousins follow in a train, one attached to the other, from tallest to smallest, each holding a bottle of fireflies like a red-hot torch, each intent on the sunken treasure in the surf.

The aunts come next, chasing the children into the choppy waves, seaweed and debris tangling their limbs. The children bop under the surface like slow-motion dancers, their muffled torches blinking while the aunts splash and scream, pulling up bunches of sea grapes and fistfuls of sand. One by one, the aunts fall into a crease of white foam curling seaward.

Suddenly she and her husband are in the heat of the moment: singers in a choir unconsciously coordinating their breathing and synchronizing their heartbeats. They dive toward the shore, toward the darkest shadows below the surface, shouting in harmony: Don't fight the currents! Don't fight the currents!

### 4.

Years later, Mari listens as her half-sister explains why they have never met before.

I could not travel, she says. I had to stay, to preserve the flowers on my brother's altar, so they never withered.

Mari leans in, fingers the silky petals of the celestinas, blue beauties from another world. The room smells sweet and sultry. It's snowing back home, the tail end of a clean white storm that delayed her trip by more than a week. She'll have to excavate her car when she returns to it, parked on the roofless deck of an airport lot.

Please, her half-sister says, don't touch these. She means the bayahibes, pink cactus roses as delicate as an infant's face.

Mari drops her hand to the edge of the altar, a side table set in a corner of her host's simple living room. There's a love seat and a rocking chair, a cocktail table on which no glass can be set because every inch is covered with family pictures in standing frames.

Outside there's traffic and reggaeton: *Que yo tengo de todo, no me falta na' / Tengo la noche que me sirve de sábana.* A thick cloud of grease and nicotine, garlic and meat, seems to hover just outside the open door where the neighbors, young and old, sit and observe them without shame. The sun is setting and their profiles blend together, the red tips of their cigarettes floating like fireflies.

Mari keeps her eyes on the altar covered with vases, candles, and a ceramic Virgin she can't identify. The boy grins back from a framed color photograph, shirtless and barefoot, sitting on the counter at Taffa's Grocery & Messenger Service. He is in his early teens, toothy and thin, and you can tell his heels are kicking the counter. All of his features are alien to her—his eyes, the knob on the nose—but there is something in the way he holds his head that feels too familiar for comfort. There are other pictures on the altar—the boy as an infant, with her half-sister at various ages, with a woman whose face Mari can't place. None of these are framed but instead curl in on themselves. Several have turned into scrolls Mari doesn't dare unfurl.

I saw you once, her half-sister says. It was your birthday and there was a party but it was raining. When I got there, to the beach, there was a minefield of broken brown beer bottles on the access road, and then so much screaming and confusion. My mother hadn't wanted me to go.

The neighbors take a breath, as audible and ghastly as an iron lung, and Mari feels her chest tighten. You must have come the year we all got caught in the riptide, she says. She remembers it only in slow motion: white water slamming her to the bottom of the ocean, burial under an avalanche so cold she thought she'd be preserved in ice forever.

My mother didn't want me to go, her half-sister says again.

Mari nods but she feels a sting of accusation.

I saw him heave you over his shoulder—it must have been you.

No, says Mari. I mean, it was quite shallow. And besides, I knew how to surrender to the tide, to stay calm, to catch a breath at every opportunity.

The half-sister's eyes narrow. What do you mean?

You know, to recognize the feel of air on my skin, to stay alive. Mari looks at the door, blocked from top to bottom by eyes and limbs and little red flares.

But it was raining that day, there was water everywhere, the half-sister says. Air and water must have been one. He dragged you out of the ocean.

Mari shrugs. She feels embarrassed. She wonders if her half-sister even knows how to swim. If any of the neighbors can float. Over the years, she's met so many islanders who rarely see the coasts. She wants to explain what it's like to know exactly what the skin of the water is like, how to rise to it with a confidence that exceeds intelligence, but the pained look on her half-sister's face silences her.

The candles on the altar flicker, black and red waves rolling and snapping on the walls. Mari hears a crackling, maybe someone opening a bag of chips outside on the stoop.

He saved you, says her half-sister. He absolutely saved you.

## 5.

Mari drives north through a blizzard, away from the airport. The little funeral flag she forgot to take off the antenna before her trip has frozen into a black cocoon. The window is down so the frigid air stings her skin. She takes a cold breath.

The GPS illustrates her trajectory—a fine burgundy line on a color screen attached to the moist inside of the windshield—but the satellite isn't working. It's a slow drive. She's maneuvering down a state route that hasn't been plowed yet, a blue highway erased from the map by the storm. On the side of the road, warning lights flash red, muffled by blankets of snow. She imagines herself traversing a tundra and that each stalled car and upturned truck is a downed mastodon or mammoth. She sees a man hacking at something. When he looks up, he yells out to her but his voice is lost in the storm.

And then she feels a current drawing her down, a familiar weight on her chest, and she remembers how she once willed herself to reach around and roll and roll and roll, pressing against the rocky bottom, twisting one arm free until she turned her hips, flipped on her belly and up to her knees, so that her head shot out of the water through a glittering, lonely plain of ice to see white lights on the horizon. She knows this is her inheritance.

# The Cola of Obliviion

The cousin's freckled arms reach out to the visitor. The cousin says she recognized her instantly from old family photos. There is glee and awkwardness, memories of what cannot possibly be remembered: playing as cherubs in the park across the street from their grandmother's house, catfish caught with handheld lines in the river behind the house.

They fill in what cannot be talked about. It's been fine, yes, except for the house (now a home for hooligans). Trouble getting meat. Fear of going to church. Secret lessons to undo the official teachings at school. And the contentment that never materialized. The cousin's husband taps his shoulder where invisible epaulets would be and pulls on an invisible beard.

They're at a tourist restaurant where the visitor will pay the bill: the cousin, the husband, their teenage daughter (the girl is the age the visitor was when she left and has a tiresome air about her), the prices in dollars, the waiter barely keeping his resentment in check.

The cousin hardly glances at the menu while her husband and daughter hide their faces behind it. The cousin says she remembers the bill of fare down to the grammatical errors, that she used to come here all the time before she got married. The husband peeks out from behind the menu. The cousin orders for her husband and their daughter: appetizers and entrees and dessert in advance. The visitor discreetly asks for a salad, for which she is teased. The waiter mumbles. The restaurant is empty but for them.

The husband orders whiskey—the enemy's drink, he says with a wink—and tells the visitor that, though she may have seen pictures of him enthusiastically jumping up and down at rallies, clapping and grinning on cue—he waits for the waiter to leave—that is not how he really feels. (The visitor has no idea what pictures he's talking about.) You get caught up in it, he says, you don't know what you're doing.

The husband makes much of the whiskey when the waiter brings it. He sniffs it, cradles it, finally sips it, then *ahhhhhs* loudly.

The daughter wants a cola—the black waters of imperialism, her father says with yet another wink as the waiter taps his foot.

It's hard to explain, says the cousin. Once, I remember, at work, they came and told us this woman,

Carmela, was a counterrevolutionary. And, you know, she had always been kind to me. She brought me crackers sometimes for the soup from the cafeteria at work because she knew I couldn't stand it, it was so watery. But they told us so that when it came time to have a meeting to repudiate her, we'd vote against her.

The waiter brings the cola, sets it down hard; it has one lonely cube floating in its center.

And we did, we voted against her, says the cousin, because she was a counterrevolutionary.

Because you get caught up in it, says the husband, so caught up you find yourself jumping up and down at the rally. You tell yourself later you did it because you were afraid someone would turn you in for not hopping on one foot . . . He laughs to himself.

So when they come and say Carmela must be expelled, separated from her work unit, naturally you raise your hand. You may as well be waving goodbye, says the cousin. And in the end, Carmela's better off anyway.

Because she was expelled and separated and forced to *not* be caught up in it, says the husband.

The waiter brings a basket of hard bread and the cousin and her husband leap to grab it before it settles on the table.

After she's expelled and separated, you realize you've done her a favor, says the cousin. By the way, the waiter forgot the butter. We need butter.

Butter! screams the daughter—who hasn't said anything at all until now. The waiter turns toward them but says nothing.

Anyway, once she was expelled and separated, Carmela couldn't do anything but leave, says the husband.

Even though she had no way to leave, says the cousin. Where's the butter?

There were mobs outside her house shouting, *Go! Go! Go!* says the husband. He breaks a hard roll in his hands, fills his mouth.

We did her the favor of freeing her from fear and shame, says the cousin.

And to discover what she was capable of, says the husband as he chews, because she had to be very strong to put up with the mobs with their *Go! Go! Go!* and throwing things.

Rotten tomatoes, says the cousin.

Pamphlets, says the husband.

Turds, says the daughter, her eyes twinkling with glee. They threw turds!

Waiter! her parents shout.

And then Carmela remembered she had a relative in Alicante and another in Zacatecas, another in Luanda, and another still in San Francisco, and a bunch in Montreal, says the cousin.

And while you're jumping up and down shouting slogans, shouting, *Go! Go! Go!* she's already settled in Miami, says the husband.

Actually, it was Madrid, that's where her postcard came from, Madrid, says the cousin. The postcard in which she thanked me for voting to expel and separate her because it was the best thing that ever happened to her, which is why I don't feel bad, because she's better off now than we are.

Can you imagine that? Better off than we are, because we were never expelled and separated.

We played by the rules.

Although, of course, we didn't want to.

But we had to.

Had to jump up and down.

And expel and separate.

Carmela abandoned us.

Like so many others.

As soon as she was settled in her new life, she forgot about us.

Didn't send us a single vitamin.

Or a throat lozenge.

Drank the cola of oblivion, says the husband.

You understand, don't you? Oh, how could you? You never lived here. They took you—have you thanked your parents for that, for taking you?

They were prescient, your parents.

But it really wasn't fair of your mother to stop speaking to us.

I understood she was Carmela's friend, of course.

But it wasn't our fault we had to jump up and down and expel and separate.

She turned her back on us, forgot about us in our hour of need.

Sometimes I think your mother thought Carmela was more important than us, her blood family.

Your mother never sent a single vitamin.

Or an analgesic.

Drank that cola.

Although I understood, in a way, because of your father.

He never got the jumping up and down.

To tell you the truth—and we're only telling you this now because you're here, and we know that means you're willing to defy him, because he can be quite the tyrant himself—he thought he was better than us because he never jumped up and down.

But he never had to!

He left before there was jumping up and down.

The food arrives all at once, including the butter and the dessert—a ball of vanilla ice cream with a string of chocolate dribbled on top. There is silence, as if in prayer, an instant in which there are sharp intakes of breath. Then there's a restrained but tense gathering of utensils and the soft hiss of a blade on meat.

After a while the husband says, Well, there was *always* jumping up and down, yes, but forced jumping up and down, no, that came later.

But your father *refused*, the cousin whispers through her teeth.

And frankly, that's why he had to be expelled and separated. What could we do?

He refused to jump, says the daughter with a certainty she can't possibly have. Do you understand? The daughter stares at the visitor, who nods, not out of agreement, but like a flagman waving runners at the end of a race.

This steak is delicious.

I want to jump up and down about this chicken, that's what I want to do right now.

If they came and asked me, I would jump up and down about this.

Not that they ask, because they don't.

They just assume you'll do it.

And, of course, you do.

Because even though they don't ask you, they make you.

Well, sometimes they ask.

But not me, says the husband, I was never asked. I just did it, because why go through all that pretense about it?

Instead of inhaling the food like they do—the mustard chicken on her mother's plate, the rare steak on her father's—the daughter hums and pushes a pair of creamy shrimp around on her dish. The ice cream bowl is empty. The salad plate too.

My daughter has never had shrimp, the cousin says by way of explanation, so she doesn't know what to do with them. She picks them off her daughter's plate and pops them in her own mouth.

Anyway, says the husband, it's not who we really are, those pictures.

Which is why you have to help us, says the cousin. Marry my husband, she proposes. I'll divorce him, you marry him, take him with you. He won't be in your way; I guarantee he won't be in your way. Later, he can reclaim our daughter. Once there, she can reclaim me. And when I get there, you can divorce him and we'll never ask anything else from you for the rest of our lives.

It's the least you can do for us, says the husband.

Your mother never sent a single vitamin, says the daughter, not a single can of meat or iPod, not a single anything.

Drank the cola, says the cousin, that terrible cola.

# WATERS

The moon simmers. I had imagined it would dance across the water in Cuba, swing gently from one wave to the other, but instead it burns, pale yellow flames blistering on the water.

I pull the black cotton T-shirt I have on away from my body. It's still dry. I can feel the soothing talc on my skin after my shower, but I know this feeling of release will be short-lived. In an hour or so, I will be damp and glowing. Unlike some other travelers—who wring the sweat out of their shirts after an afternoon walk and wheeze and worry about their hearts—I am comfortable in this state of humidity, as at home in it as if it were amniotic fluid.

It's steaming here but I still welcomed the hot water for my shower—my first in Cuba. Until I got to Isabel's house in Varadero, every shower had been more of the theoretical sort: little bursts of icy liquid from rusty showerheads in tourist hotels in Havana, or cupfuls of cold water drawn from a bucket while standing chicken-skinned in otherwise dry tubs. These experiences only added to my admiration for the Cubans who live on the island; when I rub against them on the old, tired buses or in crowded streets, they always smell sweet and fresh.

Here at Isabel's, as soon as I saw the tiny water heater in the bathroom, I begged her to light it for me. She shook her head but smiled. "All right," she said, telling me without words how unnecessary and excessive it is to take a hot shower in Cuba. "But it won't last very long," she warned, a precious match trying to catch the heater's hissing gas. Its flickering seemed to pump up the temperature. Even Isabel's brow grew moist.

In the shower, I exercised my privilege: I luxuriated under a mass of lather on my hair, felt the streams of soap running between and down my shaved and newly browned legs. I imagined the salt of the ocean from the afternoon's playful bath on the shore racing alongside the salt of my own sweat as it drained through flaky pipes and back into the land of my birth.

The day before the hot shower at Isabel's, I was invited to coffee at the home of one of Cuba's leading poets, a large, impressively built man with a long, thin, and perfectly manicured mustache in the style of the patriots from the early twentieth century. As he talked to me in his Havana home—a magnificent place with a single window offering a view of the broad boulevards that make Havana seem so French sometimes—I imagined him a man in a time warp, caught between his real existence, in which he whispered profundities with artists in open-air cafés, and ours, silently looking out at the crumbling revolutionary city, its baroque facades raked by the wind and the constant onslaught of sea salt.

The poet leaned against the windowsill. "I believe that you, of course, are a Cuban poet, a poet of the nation," he assured me, "although I do think the issue of language is very important."

We were talking in Spanish. He handed me a recent edition of one of the periodicals put out by a writers group. Like all the other publications on the island, its pages were thin and limp, as if wilted by the heat and humidity. The front page featured an essay in which the poet, contrary to everything he was saying now, drew a definitive line between Cuban writers on the island and those living abroad, regardless of whatever language they used. I thought immediately of José Martí, who wrote in a New York tenement not far from my own home.

"We must create a place for poets like you, who write in English," he said. "A Cuban place, of course, yet *different*."

"But," I said, "sometimes I write in Spanish as well."

He smiled indulgently. "Yes, I've seen what you bilingual poets do. It started with the Chicanos, didn't it?" He paused. "*Chicanos* is right, no? Or should I say *Mexican Americans*?" He looked about and giggled, as if we were sharing a terribly mischievous secret. Then he sipped noisily on his coffee.

"No," I said, "I'm not that type of bilingual poet. I write in English and Spanish, but not in the same poem."

He smiled, his fingers twisting the thin ends of his long mustache. The wind, whipping up from the streets and the ocean through the open window, ignored his work and ruffled the hair above his lip, making him look like a ferret or a mouse. "You mean, of course, that you translate into Spanish what you write in English."

I squinted and shook my head. "No, no," I said. The light was falling. "Some things come to me in English, others in Spanish. I write in whatever language it comes to me."

He nodded as if he understood. "Yes, I write some things in English too. I even have a few things in Russian, from my youth, when I spent some time studying in Moscow. That was a beautiful time."

I looked out the window and down to the street.

I spied Isabel, who had refused to come up to see the poet. "He's overrated," she'd said. "I am tired of him. But he is well connected. You should see him." She was waiting for me, her body spread out on the hood of her gray Lada, looking like someone who'd thrown herself down in an attempt at suicide. The street was deserted, otherwise she'd have drawn a crowd. The wind made her long, golden hair dance on the windshield.

"The poet's true language is the one in which he thinks," my host announced abruptly. "And you? In what language do you think?"

"It depends," I said. "Right now, I was thinking in Spanish, maybe because we're talking in Spanish. I don't know. I go back and forth, depending on who I'm with, what I'm doing."

The poet's eyebrows, pencil-thin black lines above his eyes, squiggled like an electrocardiogram. "Yes, yes, but what language do you dream in?" he demanded.

"Well," I said, "it depends. I don't always recognize the language in my dreams."

After my shower, I sit on the porch at Isabel's house trying to compose my thoughts into something coherent on the page. I've told myself I need to write every day I'm in Cuba, no matter how tired I am, how much activity there is around me. Above my head, shirts and towels flutter on a clothesline.

In the United States, I'd heard about Isabel's house mostly from friends. They told me it was on the beach, on the water at Varadero, and I had imagined something pastoral and pleasing, where I might feel the breeze off the ocean and smell the salt in the air. What no one mentioned was that there is a great expanse, a vacant lot really, between Isabel's house and the sea, and that between the lot and the water there is a highway with trucks and buses and rented cars coughing fumes, full of Argentinean and Spanish tourists throwing litter out the windows. The lot, which is apparently no one's concern, is thick with aloe, brambles, and garbage, impassable unless you're wearing long pants and hiking boots.

In the morning, we'd gone to the beach. We drove there in the Lada, fifteen minutes of maneuvering through narrow streets lined with prostitutes and illegal vendors.

"I always thought you lived *on* the beach," I said to Isabel.

She seemed confused. "I do," she said, her head nodding, as if I had somehow missed the fact that, yes, her house is right there, only a matter of yards from sand and sea.

"Well, yes." I was going to go on, to explain what

I meant, when someone tapped my arm through the car window. I turned to see a young man holding a lightbulb. He looked newly scrubbed, his hair combed back and still wet, his clothing perfectly pressed.

"Oh, we need one of those," Isabel said, reaching into the pockets of her shorts for some money.

"Here, I'll get it," I said, beating her to my bills.

I handed the young man a damp American dollar, and though all he'd heard us speak was Spanish, he responded in English. "Thank you," he said, with just the slightest accent, and dropped the lightbulb in my hand. He smiled broadly, showing a pair of missing teeth, and backed away from us and into the crowds. Isabel took the lightbulb and shook it, seemingly satisfied. The whole exchange felt odd to me, out of sync.

We piloted the Lada through the streets and into a driveway leading up to one of the newer tourist hotels. It sat on a hill, its architecture hinting of the Bahamas, with sparkling whitewashed walls, red-tiled roofs, and cozy verandas. As we drove through the resort, I noticed a sign in English that read, Mini-market. There was no Spanish translation. Another, in the shape of a small arrow pointed to a glistening lawn and read (also in English and without translation), Golf Course.

"It's not completed yet," Isabel said, as if reading

my mind. In contrast to the jammed, sweaty streets of Varadero, it was cool and empty up there.

Isabel pulled up to a designated parking space. A uniformed security guard gestured at her from a distance. "He's a friend," she said, gathering her beach towel and a pair of goggles from the backseat, explaining not just the greeting but our entry into this otherwise restricted area. "He and I went to school together."

We entered the ocean slowly, almost cautiously. Isabel had removed her shorts at the shore, but she kept her T-shirt on and now it expanded and became transparent. She wore a bathing suit with brilliant tropical colors underneath. It was low tide so I dropped to my knees to immerse myself in the water. There was nothing refreshing about it, though. It was as warm as bathwater, thick with salt and something vaguely oily on the surface. When I asked Isabel about it, she shrugged, put her goggles on, and dove in. She swam about for a minute or so, emerging with a small rock in her hand. She examined it carefully then tossed it back. I watched as she glided underwater, a ribbon of color against the sandy bottom. As she explored, I hovered, my arms outstretched, sitting in the shallow water, searching the shore for signs that this was, in fact, Varadero, and not an abandoned St. Croix.

"Hey," Isabel said, coming from behind me and putting her arms around my neck, "I'm glad you're here." She kissed me, her lips barely grazing my cheek.

"Me too," I said, holding hands with her under-water.

We are just friends but, at different times, we have been involved with the same woman, a rather reckless Don Juanita who now lives in the US and who recently dumped Isabel in favor of a former Olympic swimmer. Isabel knows about her own breakup with Don Juanita mostly through letters and friends; our mutual ex has managed to commu-nicate only indirectly.

"I'm not angry at her," she said, "but the Olym-pian, yes, I'm mad at her." She shrugged, took her goggles off, and dunked them in the oily water. She rubbed the lenses as if it mattered.

"You ready?" Isabel asks. She pokes her head out from the house, car keys in hand.

"Absolutely," I say, and close my journal. I keep starting poems I can't finish; they keep veering off, from one language to another . . .

She turns off the porch light, bright with its new bulb. A truck drives by on the highway, its groaning muffled somewhat by the ocean. Smoke rises from

its exhaust pipe and trails up to the low-hanging moon, a big yellow ball rising on the horizon.

We are on our way back to Havana for a party. I am well aware that if it weren't for me, Isabel would probably not go. She'd stay at home and read or watch American movies with Spanish subtitles on TV. But she wants me to see Havana, her city even though she lives close by in Varadero, and she wants me to have a few good stories to tell when I return to the States.

In the car, we listen to Marta Valdés and Sara Gonzáles on an MP3 player I got her for her birthday last year. The music is soft and sad, the lyrics remarkably gender-free. The car rattles but it's soothing in its own way. As we drive along, we pass a handful of other noisy cars, a couple of closed roadside snack shops, and the huge, avian shadows of oil cranes on the shores. They slowly dip and rise in silence, one after the other, for miles and miles. The car window's wide open, my elbow sticking out Cuban style, and my black T-shirt flaps like wings on my shoulders as we enter the city. The moon floats over the sea on a bed of softly percolating amber clouds.

At one of the first stoplights in Havana, we're examined from a distance by a small crowd of male and female prostitutes. The Lada, with its fading paint, is clearly local, but both Isabel and I mystify them: though her clothes and body language correspond to the languorous way of the island, she is blond and wears glasses with yellow and black frames (a gift from another New York friend, and too fashionable for Cuba); there's too much burnt red under my tanned skin, and my clothes—all dark colors—do not suit Cuba's heat and humidity.

At the stoplight, I lift my camera to my eye and focus and, as if on cue, the prostitutes descend. The first is a sinewy boy in his late teens, henna-skinned and perfect but for the gold tooth that appears when he smiles.

"Señorita," he says, doing his best Latin Romeo imitation, "perhaps you would like a little company tonight, no?" He affects an Iberian accent, taking a chance that I'm a Spanish tourist and might be amused by his attempt at sounding like a compatriot. He leans into the car window and with him comes a waft of soap and cologne.

"She's already got company for tonight," Isabel says a bit too quickly, too protectively, in her own open-mouthed Cuban Spanish.

"Ah," he says, still holding on to the car, but waving over two young girls with his other arm. "Then perhaps you'd like to make it a party, eh?" He's looking at me but talking to Isabel, unsure where I'm from or whether I understand. His gold tooth sparkles. "This is Nancy," he says, pushing one of the girls up to the window. She's no more than eighteen, her eyes encircled with heavy black liner and fatigue. "And this is Mayra," he says, grabbing the other girl by the arm. This one is golden and resentful, her lips curling.

"Encantada," I say.

Isabel rolls her eyes. The light has changed. The other cars are involved in their own transactions or going around us, the drivers indifferent to the scene.

"Ah, you're from Miami," says the boy, understanding my accent as native but my demeanor as foreign.

"No, from New York," I say, smiling at them.

"Mayra has a cousin in New York," he says, yanking her up closer.

She shakes him off. "Ya, coño," she says, resisting. She's not much older than Nancy, her face still round and babyish under all the makeup.

"We can show you Havana," the boy says, "a private Havana, a Havana especially for you."

An exasperated Isabel shakes her head, tells him no. He leans in, his whole head inside the Lada now. I'm blinded by his gold tooth so I push myself back, giving him room to continue his sales pitch to Isabel, who I know won't be moved.

I look out the car window to Mayra, who's standing out on the street, her arms folded stubbornly across her chest. She stares back at me, full of pride and hate.

The party's in an old, majestic but dilapidated mansion in the Vedado neighborhood. It's a colorless, muddy shade but I can see its former elegance in the chipped columns at the front, the scalloped borders on the doors. A young girl sits in front with a metal cashbox on her lap. She asks for ten pesos—not even a dollar. I give her a few American bills and Isabel and I enter through the large wooden doors that seem to open just for us.

Inside there are a crush of bodies, revolving disco balls, and a suffocating humidity. It's wall to wall flesh, all of it drenched and yearning. I smell talcum and sex, perfume and menstrual blood. It takes a minute for me to adjust my senses. There is a dizzying disco song blasting from the speakers—coffin-sized boxes hang from chains on the ceiling; paint flakes down like confetti.

As the partygoers come into view, I see men and women pressed up against each other, men rubbing naked nipples against other men, women gyrating between pairs of men who encourage them with grins and long, snaky tongues that dart in and out of their purple mouths. Shirts and blouses are trans-lucent, second skins sticking to breasts and bones.

In one corner, I see a black figure separate into two silhouettes, long dark hair soaked and fused to their naked shoulders. "I want their picture!" I shout to Isabel above the noise, pointing. She has her finger around a loop in my jeans, making sure we don't lose each other. She follows me as I approach the lovers.

"Con permiso," I say in my loudest voice, al-though I can tell from the way they're looking at my mouth that they are lipreading. "Listen, I'm a writer—a poet—from New York and I wonder if you'd mind if I took your picture?" What I mean is, I want their image to inspire me. I want to print these up and fill my New York space with so much Havana that I can project myself back here anytime. I lift my camera for them to see.

They are both gorgeous, olive-hued, with dark, wounded eyes and creamy skin. The smaller one turns away and folds into her lover, who looks at me with a sober and unforgiving expression. "We would mind very much," she says. I hear her slightly accented English through the crunching sounds of some German industrial dance song, dismissing the fact that I spoke to her in Spanish.

"Aaaayyyyyyyy, take my picture, take my pic-ture!" shouts an excited young queen dripping with faux pearls who drags his drunken lover into my face.

I laugh and nod, bring the camera up, and push the button. The flash explodes, freezing everyone for a split second. Faces turn toward us, some excited, others placid, some enraged. The beautiful women are gone.

"Mi amor, photograph us!" says a boy in a sailor's suit, pushing his companion, a soldier in full military regalia, at me.

Isabel puts her hands squarely on my hips and drives me away, through the labyrinth of flesh out to a patio, where the air is suddenly cool and refreshing. We pass a small table, where greasy paper plates pile up, and a cart full of rapidly melting ice from which a couple of lithe young men are selling beer and soda. We settle under a low-hanging tree with ripe, aromatic leaves. The moon is somewhere high above us.

"Jesus," I say, laughing, "what is it about gay men, huh? It doesn't matter where in the world I go, they're always listening to disco, they always want their picture taken."

Isabel pulls a handkerchief from her pocket; she wipes her face and sighs. "Good party?" she asks.

I nod. "Yeah, and an amazing place," I say, surveying the mansion. The owners have cleared the front room of all furniture and blocked access to the other rooms. There are meaty men standing guard in front of the doors leading to the bedrooms and kitchen. Some of the windows that look out to the patio are boarded up, nailed shut, but we can see the glow of a light inside one of them and a solitary shadow in a rocking chair, reading a newspaper.

"That must be the mother. Listen," Isabel says, coming closer to me. Her breath is hot on my face. "No more pictures here, okay?"

"Yeah?"

She shrugs. "Yeah, you know . . . the flash." I know it's more than that, but it's okay.

Then a short brown-skinned woman comes over to us. She's wearing a red suit, with a lacy red shirt and a red ribbon holding her hair in a curly wet ponytail. Her apparel is sort of corporate femmy, but her demeanor is entirely butch. As she crosses the patio, she's practically marching.

"Tú—mujer linda," she says, pointing to me. Her smile is sly, cocky. "Quieres bailar?"

There's an unintelligible rap song booming through the speakers now, which seem nearly as powerful out here as inside the house. I see Isabel in my peripheral vision, smirking at my little admirer. I tower over this girl.

"Maybe later," I say, "something slower."

Isabel smiles, nods approvingly at my discretion.

But suddenly the music shifts. The beat is tropical and lazy. "J'imanije . . ." sings an indolent, Caribbean voice.

"Ay, mamita, si es una canción francesa," says the little butch, imploring.

Isabel laughs. "That's not French," she tells her, "it's some kind of Creole."

"You're not together, are you?" the girl asks, as if it just occurred to her.

Instinctively, we both shake our heads. The red-dressed butch grabs my hand with her moist, slippery fingers and pulls. "Vamos," she says, and I obey, laughing over my shoulder at Isabel, who seems entertained by the turn of events.

On the dance floor, we are overwhelmed by the long, gangly bodies that sway dreamily around us. A few women wrap themselves around each other, their bodies cloaked in shiny perspiration. My dancing partner pulls me toward her with one swift, hard tug, but I resist. I feel my T-shirt molding to my back, as soaked as if I'd been standing out in the rain. We struggle wordlessly back and forth until we come to a compromise: I nail my elbows to the inside of hers and her hand goes to the small of my back and works from there. All the while, she sings, "J'imanije . . ." In my head, I make it French: "J'imagine." As we turn, I catch Isabel's eye. She's leaning up against a wall, watching us and smiling. She's drinking a beer I don't remember her buying.

When the song ends, my partner doesn't give me a chance. As soon as the notes of the new tune begin—something even slower, even more drippily romantic—she takes advantage of the instant I relax to yank me into her. My breasts squish up against her chest, hers slide around under mine. My nose is in her hair, which smells of roses. She sings, her voice raspy but strong, directed at my ear. I feel her flushed breath on my lobe and neck. I think I recognize the song—something by Marta Valdés?—but I can't make out the words.

And now she seems more convincing, leading me, turning us in small, tight circles. The room spins, like a ride at an amusement park. I look for Isabel, but all the faces have smudged together. I try to pull away but I can't. It's as if all the air has been siphoned out of the space between our bodies and we're being held together by suction. The little butch continues to sing, her tone rising with the song's crescendo, her throat full of emotion.

It's then I look up and see Mayra, the girl from the intersection. She's framed by a pair of couples whose deliberate moves make them look as if they're peaking in slow motion. She is across the room, standing in a thin funnel of light, her shirt loose around her candied shoulders, barely damp, but her full lips glisten, even at a distance. Her eyes are bright and she's smiling, free and open. She doesn't recognize me as the foreigner from the stoplight. She waves at me as if we're old friends, perhaps neighbors. I feel something loosen and drop inside me.

I jerk away from my dancing partner, who falls back, disoriented by my sudden determination. The disco ball spins aquamarine.

Mayra's eyes open wide; she's laughing now, her head tossed back languidly against the wall. She mouths something to me. I have no idea what language she's speaking. But, wet and feverish, I slowly begin to make my way toward her.

# Supermán

They say that, for the longest time, Enrique didn't know he was a superman. What he understood was that men liked his dick. He'd known it since he was a boy, when an older neighbor had kiddingly pushed him into the water off the Malecón and stared at the wet outline of his member after they dragged themselves laughing up to the rocks. What the hell is that? he'd asked, not waiting for an answer and grabbing it with his big hand through the fabric of the boy's shorts. The neighbor was too quick, and the tug too electrifying, so that the boy couldn't hide the swelling of his penis in the man's fist. Behind them, up past the Malecón's long wall, car horns blew like Haydn's trumpets. The neighbor pushed him roughly to the edge of the rocks then silently instructed him to sit with his legs in the water and his back to the traffic. The neighbor submerged himself and brought his head between the boy's thighs. He popped his fly and pushed as much as he could into his mouth before spitting it back out. It's an eel, he said, it's too much for me. Seeing the boy's panicked look, the neighbor said, Don't worry, don't worry, and curled his fingers, pushing and pulling until, many minutes later, the boy finally shot over his head and into the waters.

As they were making their way back across the reef to the Malecón, the neighbor shook his hand out and joked about how it had almost fallen asleep. Embarrassed, the boy apologized but the neighbor clapped him on the back. That's gonna make you a lot of money, my friend, just you wait. The neighbor, whose name was Osmany, grinned the whole way home.

They say that was the beginning—that then Osmany told Mercedes, his wife, about the sleepy-eyed neighbor boy, how his penis went on for so long it seemed to defy human possibility. She had him come by their apartment and, after fussing over him so much that he began to tremble, he was finally convinced to unbutton his pants and show her—except this time, his treasure lay flat and soft on his thigh, still impressive but inert. She shook her head in dismay.

Hmm, said Osmany, who was baffled: he couldn't swallow that thing, much less let it up his ass; the boy was too young to fuck and yet there was something in his somnambulant gaze that let Osmany know trying to get the boy to take a dick in his mouth—a mouth like syrup, glistening and sweet—would be futile. That strange boy seemed so different from mortal men.

They say Osmany was a valet at a downtown hotel and he'd see the boy each morning on the way to work, just lingering on the steps of the Saint Jude Thaddeus Church on the corner of San Nicolás and Tenerife. He'd wave and the boy would nod, his eyes so heavy-lidded you'd have thought he'd just woken up on those steps: shirtless, flawless. Sometimes he'd be eating an orange, delicately biting the golden half-moons, and other times he'd sprint across the street at the sound of a woman's voice and disappear inside the building. In the afternoon, when he came home for lunch, Osmany would see him hanging over one of the second-floor balconies or back on the church steps reading the newspaper.

Oh, for the love of God, just invite him over again, Mercedes said.

They say that's when it became routine for the boy to visit in the evening, always barefoot, to have a snack or dinner with the young couple. Sometimes he'd stick around to watch them have sex. Initially, Osmany had thought they'd try to bring him into their lovemaking (Mercedes would make him wash his feet first), but while the boy was willing to be kissed, he wasn't much of a kisser, and while he was game to be stroked, he wasn't enthusiastic about re-

ciprocation. In fact, most of the time he wasn't particularly aroused by their efforts and would just curl
up and go to sleep.

It was Mercedes who noticed it was only once
they'd given up engaging him and focused on enjoying themselves that the boy would come to life. Then
he'd stare at Osmany's member as it slid in and out
of Mercedes and his own would grow and grow and
grow. Osmany reached for it one time but Mercedes
grabbed his wrist. Don't touch it, she whispered,
and let's see what he does. But the boy did nothing,
or at least nothing of the usual sort. Instead, he'd use
his powerful thighs to bounce the shiny mast from
one leg to the other, which sent Osmany and Mercedes into a frenzy.

Did the boy have a family? Some say he was
an orphan, a street kid. Others were sure he lived
with his mother and a handful of siblings; still others say he was an only and much treasured child. A
few reported that both his parents lived in that
upstairs apartment in Los Sitios across from the
church. His mother (or an aunt, or an older sister—
it was unclear) was a washerwoman, or a wait-
ress, maybe a receptionist at a clinic in Vedado, but
the father was sickly and so was never seen or heard
from, which explained why the boy seemed to flutter
about without aim. Some insisted the father was a

junkie who only showed up during bouts of sobriety.

Whatever his true beginnings, all the origin stories began and ended in Los Sitios, with the boy sitting on the church steps. Did he go to school? Certainly for a while, but who knows when he dropped out. He could read, this was plain—not just from his extended focus on the newspaper he managed to get hold of every day, but also in his choice of reading material: dime novels, especially translated American pulp Westerns. There was always one in his back pocket.

Years later—yes, years, that's how much Osmany and Mercedes invested in the boy—they put together a little show in their living room for a group of special friends. The windows were shuttered, lights dimmed, cold beer and aloe were passed out to the handful of guests who sat sweating in a half-circle facing the couch. And there was the kid, bare-chested and barefoot, in trousers with rolled cuffs. From above, a lamp provided a spotlight.

When the kid fished his member from inside his pants, it curled like the neck on the Loch Ness Monster. The room gasped, and then came the sounds of zippers, fabric rustling, and heavy breathing. Behind the half-circle of seats, standing with Mercedes's back to him, Osmany lifted her dress to reveal the round of her buttocks. The kid's penis wrenched itself to attention. It looked like a torpedo searching for targets. The guests panted and struggled as Osmany pressed his own erection into his wife's rear. The kid thrust his hips up, then reached into his trousers again, this time to give his testicles some air. By the time he orgasmed—an act perpetrated by telepathy between him and the couple in the back of the room so that he never, ever so much as flicked his wrist—the men in the room were grunting and crying. One had dropped to his knees, but Osmany pulled him back by the shirt collar as if he were on a leash, and the man lowered his head and licked the floor.

They say one of the guests in that room was a friend of José Orozco García, the owner of the Shanghai Theater in Chinatown, a burlesque house with about seven hundred seats on the main floor and another three hundred and fifty in the balcony. The Shanghai hosted live shows and a handful of films each day. They say that Orozco's friend rushed to tell him what he'd seen and the next thing they knew, the kid—now tall and athletic, though still sleepy-eyed and barefoot (it was his preference)—was strolling down Zanja Street with Osmany, serious cash in their pockets in anticipation of his stardom.

And it came, that stardom, and with it his new name: Supermán. An unseen harp would play a kind of roll, and then a brass section would introduce him with a short triad-based motif. He'd float onstage like Tathagata, his smoothly proportioned body covered in a flowing red cape. Then he'd pivot to profile and reveal his magnificence. Afterward, he'd sit on his throne and will his way to rapture.

Some say Supermán was a sensation right away. Others that it took some time: the kid didn't know what to make of the light in his eyes or the black mouth of the theater that seemed to want to swallow him whole. He had to learn to surrender, to find a place inside himself where he was alone, where he could conjure what he needed to bring himself to peak. Still others claim to remember seeing Osmany in the wings—sometimes with Mercedes and sometimes with another woman or man—playing out what he knew fueled the Shanghai's new star.

They say Supermán's member was ten, twelve, even eighteen inches long, though there are some who insist it only seemed so hefty because of the play of lights in the theater. They say they were masters of forced perspective at the Shanghai, that they dusted his thighs and scrotum with a blue tint and covered his penis with an orange gel so it would give the impression of greater weight and length. A few say that when Supermán turned to show his treasure, what the audience saw was the forearm of a dwarf concealed at his side, his fist held to project a shadow that looked like a stout head. Some insisted it really was that long, and that, more importantly, he was able to pull it up without touching, so that it always seemed charged and ready. On certain nights, and only for special shows, Supermán would earn his name by attaching himself to a wire that was hooked to a contraption on the Shanghai ceiling that would hurl him above the heads of men and women who would jump from their seats, hands grasping in the air, laughing and sucking their knuckles.

Oh, those were easy days. They say Supermán bought himself white gabardine suits and comfortable custom-made leather sandals for when there was no choice but to cover his feet. He bought serious hardcover books he lined up next to his bed and dined out with friends from the neighborhood. He thought about buying a car but realized he'd have to learn to drive, and besides, he found the nightly walk to the Shanghai invigorating. Mercedes suggested he was making enough to move out of Los Sitios, that he could probably find bigger and better quarters for himself (and his family?) in Vedado or Old Havana, but even then it was clear Supermán understood his activities would not be seen with the same kindness in other places. (And Osmany agreed with Supermán: That's a machete in your pants, he said, and this—he tapped his forearm to indicate color—this is trouble. That—now pointing at his crotch—will only make it worse. Better to stay where everyone already knows you.)

No worries, I'm going to live here forever, Supermán told Mercedes, but she scoffed. She and Osmany were already making plans to relocate to Vedado with their percentage of his earnings, though into two different apartments: Mercedes had fallen in love with one of the strippers at the Shanghai and was moving in with her.

I'm going to live here forever and ever, Supermán insisted.

They laughed, but he meant it. He got a big garbage can to put right at the corner of the church, bought flowers for the women who'd seen him grow up and now enjoyed watching him strut off to work in the evening, and shooed the boys peeing against the sacellum walls in the early hours when he got home. Everyone says Supermán was as much a hero at home as in the spotlight.

In those days, tourists filled the streets and the seats at the Shanghai, and Supermán was applauded and adored every night. But not all was wonderful: now and then there were shots heard in the early hours, and once, walking home in the morning light, Supermán stumbled on a man whose chest had been ripped apart by a burst of bullets. He read the papers; he knew what was going on. But still he threw off his shoes and ran home, closing the doors of the balcony overlooking Saint Jude Thaddeus, dropping his mattress onto the floor so that if bullets came through his windows or doors, they'd whiz above his head.

Having no professional responsibilities other than to sit and meditate, Supermán didn't have to attend the afternoon rehearsals at the Shanghai, though he often went by and hung out with the girls who supervised the day-care circle. There was one he liked a lot named Gise, the eldest daughter of one of the other performers (a beautiful smoky woman whose specialty was sucking off another performer while hanging upside down). Gise watched over the cast members' kids and flirted with him. She was almond-eyed, with a mischievous glint that sparked the sleepy Supermán.

Some people say it wasn't long before they took up together, but that their affair was doomed from the start. They say they made love once, a gingerly act full of possibility, but when Supermán took to his throne that night, his penis dropped like a spooked marsupial. No amount of recall, no effort to focus, proved useful. He resorted to petting and coaxing, but his panic only fueled more panic: in the audience, restlessness led to outrage. There were insults and denunciations, a shower of coins, and then a shoe hit Supermán in the face. He collected his goods with both hands, enveloped himself in his cape, and scrambled off stage, panting as a line of showgirls—including Gise's mother—ran onstage to shake their naked breasts.

They say Osmany and Mercedes gave him a talking-to that night (or maybe it was Orozco himself, or any one of the others at the Shanghai, maybe even Gulliver the dwarf). You have to make a world simply from wanting, find fulfillment beyond your own delectation, said whoever took him aside. On this path you must become a monk of mortification.

Oh, you go ahead and keep your juice! That's what Gise exclaimed, but it was in dismay, maybe even in mockery (or so goes at least one story).

Some say she never talked to him again, that his refusal to consider becoming a gardener or bricklayer, a clerk or a driver, sealed it for her: she'd grown up at the Shanghai and, though the experience had not been unpleasant, she was not interested in repeating it for any of her own kids to come. Her mother had carefully cultivated her future respectability with private school tuition and trips to Key West, Florida, where she met educated Bahamians and second-and third-generation Cubans who'd never heard of the

Shanghai, or thought it was a myth. Her mother aspired to a different kind of man for her, a man who owned his own car, who had a trade or profession, no matter how dull, and who would love and protect her golden girl. What do you want to be? Gise asked Supermán. What do you want to do with your life?

Others say Supermán and Gise defied everyone and stayed together in mutual suffering. Always on the precipice, always embracing denial to the point that they both experienced lacerating muscle pain and, sometimes, even hallucinations. There were nights when Supermán couldn't control the flood and Gise would weep with joy and roll in the froth on the wet sheets like a baby seal. Others say it wasn't that way at all, that the two found their own naive path to coitus reservatus, and Supermán would breathe slow and deep and use a steely stillness to lift her to heaven. In his mind—and maybe in hers too—together they would become a glowing ball of light.

What's known for sure is that one evening Supermán showed up for work and found the Shanghai's back door shuttered. When he rounded the theater, he saw Orozco (or Gulliver or one of the other workers) placing a lock and chain on the front entrance. It was drizzling and Supermán held a folded newspaper above him to keep his cottony head dry.

We're closed, the shutterer (whomever it was)

said. We only close for revolution, so come back when it's over.

On the way home the skies were gray, the streets were deadly quiet, and the only faces Supermán saw were wide-eyed behind a flutter of curtains. At some point there was a shattering sound—a gunshot or a car backfiring—and it felt like a punch to the gut. For weeks after his dismissal, Supermán kept going back to the Shanghai, spied the lock on the door, and slinked away.

Did he go back to Gise and tell her they could wait it out, that they could let go, enjoy themselves fully, and discover too late she liked it best when he was the monk of mortification? Did he return to tell her he'd keep her safe and find her mother had spirited them both away to Key West or New York or maybe even Paris, to a new life in exile from which neither would ever return? Or did he go back to her and, now that he had her every day, realize he could never cool off, that no matter how much he sweat, the glowing ball of light had become an eternal and consuming flame? Did he learn to cultivate white ginger flowers and sell them for bridal bouquets, funeral wreaths, or offerings to the saints? Or was he frying eggs and stirring rice in a steaming kitchen somewhere? Maybe he was at home, at his father's bedside (or his mother's, or grandmother's, or that of the older sister who always believed in him), tending to him or her until their last breath? Maybe he begged Orozco to talk to somebody and ended up hauling bags of sugar down at the ports. There were Americans in Havana Bay, Americans in the bars, Americans in the capitol building. Did he root out Osmany and Mercedes and her lover and put on private shows? Or did he lean on the walls of Saint Jude Thaddeus after dusk, loosen his fly, and let men drop to their knees, surrendering whatever was in their pockets, just so he could eat?

Those were dark days, very dark days that turned into years. After the clarion of revolution and the drudgery of dictatorship, he found himself alone. And then, just as suddenly and unexpectedly, the skies parted and the sunshine of democracy returned: the Shanghai's doors swung open and there was Supermán, as drowsy as ever, in one of his gabardine suits, barefoot again, anxiously tapping a rolled newspaper against his thigh while waiting for Orozco to recognize him. And he did—he did! Who could forget? And of course he had work for him, but this time it would be different. This time Supermán would have a part in the show. This time Supermán would come to rehearsals, he would be in the cast. And Supermán accepted, because what else could he do? One thing he'd discovered in the few years away from the

Shanghai was the curse of his peculiar talent. It had been so easy for him to ascend from Shodan to Judan in his profession that he'd never considered anything else. Wherever he was, whatever he'd done to survive during his time in the wilderness, the experience had shown him that maybe, just maybe, he'd sealed his fate, that whatever window of opportunity Gise had tried to open was now shut.

Come by tomorrow at three o'clock, said a beaming Orozco, and Supermán arrived at two thirty, bathed and perfumed, dressed in crisp and clean clothes, a clutch of white ginger flowers for whoever might be his partner.

*Señoras y señores, ladies and gentlemen . . . bienvenidos al teatro más espectacular del mundo. El Gran Teatro Sanghai, una gloria de Cuba. Aquí no paramos nunca, aunque se la paramos a cualquiera!*

And then it was that way every day, followed by dinner and performances at nine thirty and eleven thirty. After that, the occasional private show, sometimes at the San Francisco brothel, the Mambo Club, or at a gangster's private party, usually at one or three or five in the morning.

At the Shanghai, the script was simple: The audience would see a couple walk into a restaurant and sit at a table, then Supermán would come to take their order. They'd joke about the tenderness of the meat and she'd order coffee, Supermán's cue to ask if she wanted some *cream* with that. Later, there was a different skit: a woman (whenever possible, her skin a contrast to his) would be tied to a stake and he'd appear, caped and menacing, to rape her. This particular skit was a big hit (it was even referenced in an American movie), and included a lot of his trademark moves, such as the pivot to profile and the long streams of cum that would arc high and thick in the air. (As time went by, he stopped this and made virtue of his stamina instead.)

They say it was more or less then that he decided to attend to his talent, to cultivate the lightning that ran through his body. There are those who claim to have witnessed him in a trance that lasted hours, never once flagging, never once touching himself, his face still, his eyes blank as if he were hypnotized. Some say if you sat close to the stage or used opera glasses, you could see the most subtle of movements, a ripple of radiance up his spine, like a river navigating the force of the current. They say he never smiled, never grimaced, but seemed to have a sixth sense, both for his partners' threshold and for how far he could push those watching.

Soon Supermán had regained and then surpassed his previous fame, and the rape scene would be followed by an offer to the handful of women in the audience to come and ride his magic wand. There would always be at least one taker, a girl from Boise or Louisiana, sometimes Los Angeles or Maine, giggly and scared but so excited: in those days, Havana was a place where conscience took a holiday.

The city was rich and opulent then, with Nat King Cole at the Tropicana; rumba dancers at the Zombie Club; casinos at the Nacional, Montmartre, and the Sans Souci; the Cabaret Kursal and the Palette Club. Ernest Hemingway held court at La Floridita, and elsewhere Edith Piaf, Jimmy Durante, Maurice Chevalier, and Frank Sinatra rioted until the wee hours.

Sinatra, in fact, was a regular at the Shanghai, where he sometimes brought the beautiful Ava Gardner. And it's told—it's been written about, even in the official press—that one evening Gardner went alone and asked to meet Supermán after the show. They say he was in a robe in his dressing room, reading one of those pocket Westerns, when Gulliver opened the door without knocking and breathlessly announced she was on her way up. Supermán didn't move. When Gulliver escorted her in, he lifted his lids and made a barely perceptible nod in her direction. She asked his name, his real name, and told him to use it later when he came by her suite at the Hotel Nacional. Then she stepped up, brushed the Western aside, and opened his robe. She ran her hand down the inside of his thigh and shivered. To Gulliver's surprise—and it's hard to know if this is his direct testimony or second-, third-, or tenthhand— Enrique removed her palm, closed his robe, and let his eyes drop back to his novel.

Yes, it's true, no one saw him come in or out of the hotel, but later that same night, the Barefoot Contessa was rushed by ambulance to the Hospital Calixto García, delirious, with blood between her legs. Sinatra, who was buddies with the mafiosos who ran Havana, swore revenge, but Enrique's own criminal friendships—his value as entertainment and talisman—trumped even Ol' Blue Eyes. (Others say it was a belligerent Sinatra himself who beat her and then sought to blame it on Enrique, for all the obvious reasons. Many will insist Enrique always denied ever being alone with her.)

Yes, Enrique had gotten into the spirit of things by then: He would go out with the mobsters who ran most of the establishments where he worked, party with them and their hangers-on until dawn (though it's said he never drank, and never smoked more than the occasional cigarette). He now wore linen suits, starched shirts, or tight pullovers that showed off his muscles, though he never quite took to shoes. He told stories and jokes, and sometimes he'd chat about movies or even books. Mostly, though, he listened: he nodded that almost invisible nod, he made direct and sustained eye contact, he knew when to pat men on the back or squeeze a thigh (it depended on the man) and when to whisper to a woman so his lips brushed her ear. Of course, he performed acrobatics and endurance marathons for the highest bidders. (Some said he fucked mules onstage, others said it was bulls, and only for private clients, but none of that was true—those were the rumored deeds of another man, known as El Toro.)

In Los Sitios they still talk about the wild shindigs Enrique hosted, about the drums and the screaming, the men pissing off the second-floor balcony and passing out on the steps of Saint Jude Thaddeus. Did the neighbors mind the noise, the debauchery? No, not at all—everyone knew what Enrique did for a living, and he was generous: a dress for a quinceañera, dentures for a grandmother, a new coat of paint for Saint Jude Thaddeus. He brought visible and speedy help, consolation for the suffering of his neighbors and patience for their whims. No kid in Los Sitios lacked a cake on his or her birthday.

Still, there are others who refute these stories, who say Enrique drew a line around his home in Los Sitios as a kind of fortress of solitude and that only later, much later, did he come to share it with a partner, and even then, they were so quiet and circumspect that if you didn't already know, you never would.

Not that there weren't occasions when Enrique's worlds came together against his will, like the time Marlon Brando wouldn't leave him alone. This was a swaggering post-Oscar Brando, a Brando who'd recently pranced through a fake Havana for the cameras and now wanted to experience the real thing. He'd stepped into the Shanghai with two girls, one on each arm (they say these were dancers from the Tropicana, but they could have been from anywhere), watched the show, and demanded to meet its legendary star. He caught up with him in the same dressing room where Ava Gardner had come calling. This time, Enrique was at a small table slicing strawberries (each the size of an egg) when Gulliver opened the door. On his left at the table was a copy of Colin Wilson's *The Outsider* and on his right an English-Spanish dictionary held open by a rock. He looked up with his droopy eyes and saw the world's most famous actor before him, with his weight-lifter arms and Charles Atlas chest. It was hot, very hot, in that dressing room, and sweat beaded up almost immediately on Brando's broad high forehead then rolled down his flushed untough cheeks.

When Gulliver left, he took the distraught show-girls with him. They say he came back later, pressed his ear to the door, and heard Brando talking, that he figured out later the long pauses must have been when one or the other would look for a word in the dictionary, and then Enrique would repeat it back and Brando would say, Yeah, yeah, that's it, and Enrique would say, Good, very good, in only slightly accented English (one of the side effects of so much exposure to tourists).

Sensitive people are so vulnerable, Brando supposedly told Enrique. They're so easily brutalized and hurt just because they are sensitive. A sensitive person receives fifty impressions when somebody else may only get seven. The more sensitive you are, the more certain you are to be brutalized. Then you never allow yourself to feel anything, because you always feel too much.

Some people say Enrique gave Brando the wildest, scariest night of his life, then deposited him back at the Nacional the following afternoon, jaundiced and sick. But others—especially those who rely on Gulliver as a source—say that's not what happened at all. They say instead Brando fell in love, that he followed Enrique home, that he offered to take him with him, back to Hollywood, then to Japan where he was scheduled to film his next picture.

Others say a jealous lover ushered Brando away, but the neighbors themselves—the neighbors who for days collected the movie star's autograph and borrowed cameras for pictures with him on his rented motorbike—insist it was Enrique la Reina who looked up at him with his sleepy gaze and said: I'm going to live here forever. On the last day, a weeping Brando was seen motoring away, *The Outsider* in his back pocket.

After that, life seemed to just go on for Enrique la Reina: sleeping during the day, reading and cooking in the afternoon, shows at night and in the wee hours. There were loves, of course, but no one knows—not really—who they were, how long they lasted. It's possible he was partnered when they began to hear about bombings in the city, when stepping out for any errand could make him a witness to the aftermath of any of these attacks. He bought rebel bonds, or maybe not. He observed the groups of workers at the Shanghai arguing the merits of Revolution (because this was a big-R Revolution, everyone knew that).

So it was no surprise when he came to work one day and discovered yet again that the Shanghai had been shuttered. Come back after the Revolution, Orozco (or whoever) told him again, smiling, but it was an anxious smile, a smile with a tic. The hand that put up the *Closed* sign trembled.

The Shanghai stars—the dancers, the sex artists, the choreographers and lighting technicians, the

projectionists, the carpenters, the makeup and cos-
tume artists—were adrift now. Who would remember them? Who would tell their story? For years the
Shanghai's biggest star had banned cameras, refused
to pose for postcards, and generally avoided the
press. He'd always understood his legend depended
on mystery, on personal experience. And now, a law-
yer for one of the mobsters wanted to make a film,
before he disappeared.

Do it for history, Gulliver told him.

Somewhere in Florida, and maybe in New York,
that grainy celluloid gives a glimpse of Supermán's
glory, but it's just a glimpse, a god in his twilight,
unabashedly naked but for a pair of black socks:
there is no ceremony, no performance, just evidence
the way it might be presented at trial.

What happened to Supermán?

A writer who lives on San Lázaro says Supermán
lives in Havana still, on that same street, a shriveled
old man in a wheelchair, his legs and testicles lost
to diabetes. He says his wife—maybe Gise, maybe
someone else—takes care of him to this day and that
the kids in the neighborhood pass him with no idea
of who he once was. He says Supermán sits on his
stoop—there's no ramp, there's no going anywhere
without help—and watches the human parade as if
he were back in Los Sitios.

Another writer—this one a crime reporter in Mexico City—says that's not true, that Supermán got out of Cuba in the early days of the Revolution, that he made it to Mexico City. She says he was trying to find a way to Miami, or over the border to Texas, when he was stabbed to death, neither an accident nor a coincidence, given that Sinatra—who'd never forfeited his right to avenge Ava Gardner—was in town for a few charity concerts.

Others say he made it out of Cuba and landed in the Jim Crow South, a shock so severe he drank himself to death, or was lynched, or left to die on the ramp to the emergency room of a whites-only hospital after a terrible beating or car accident. A story went around for a while that he joined the army and went back to the island as a CIA operative during the Bay of Pigs invasion and then later served in the capture and interrogation of Che Guevara in Bolivia, but there was scant evidence to so much as suggest any of that. There was a rumor, too, that he was one of the Watergate burglars, but that was quickly discounted. Still others claimed intermittent sightings in Havana for almost two decades, and that he only got away when he slipped onto a barge during the Mariel crisis.

A few say he became a doorman in Manhattan, detached and polite, though others say he lived off disability as soon as his refugee benefits ran out. They say he suffered from AIDS-related dementia and died by his own hand sometime in the nineties after leaving behind a long letter blaming Fidel Castro, his own personal Doomsday, for his demise. There are reports of paramedics wearing long yellow gloves as they brought him out on a stretcher from a Bronx tenement into the bright light of a cold winter day.

Others testify they saw Enrique in San Francisco in the late sixties, happily buying Victorians in Haight-Ashbury. A few claim he migrated to Neptune, New Jersey, where a long-lost cousin helped him set up a little café he ran with measured success until his retirement. One alleged witness says he talked to him when he was a school janitor in Tampa, married to a third- or fourth-generation Cuban, a deaf woman who owned a beauty salon. Between her kids from a prior marriage and the ones she had with him, they raised seven success stories. Someone else reported he was one of the big donors against the antigay brouhaha raised by Anita Bryant in Miami so long ago. Another says he made it all the way to Egypt, where he worked for years as a guide at the pyramids.

What's true is he's as gone as Amelia Earhart or Matias Pérez—except in Los Sitios. There, the writing on the walls continues to call out his name, to-day and maybe forever: *Viva Supermán!*

# THE MALDIVES

As soon as I was diagnosed with a brain tumor, I knew I wanted to be here, in the Maldives. My tumor is benign, at least technically, just a little drop of fat, not cancerous. It's growing about one centimeter a year, which is about the same as the rising sea level in the Maldives. But this coincidence isn't what drew me to these islands.

For me, everything started just before I left Cuba. I'd just scored an American visa because my father, who'd escaped years before on a raft, had filed for me under a family reunification provision of US asylum laws. Not that my father had much interest in being reunited with me: when he'd lived in Cuba, he'd never hesitated to tell me I was a punishment from God.

I'd ask him, For what? What did you do to deserve me? It must have been pretty bad.

But he'd just shake his head and walk away. I'm not going to confess to you, he'd spit over his shoulder.

Years later, all settled in San Francisco with a new Mexican wife and a revved-up religious calling that involved marching up and down Market Street passing out pamphlets urging homosexuals to repent, he decided maybe God would be more convinced of his commitment and sacrifice if he saved his own daughter first.

And I was ready to be saved. Not from homosexuality, but from the boredom of Havana. Oh, I know, most Americans hear Havana and think Tropicana and classic cars, parties and salsa, even though salsa is Puerto Rican. But for a Cuban like me, Havana means living with several generations in a crowded three-room apartment (in my case: my mother, her boyfriend, my grandmother and her boyfriend, my sister and her boyfriend, my nineteen-year-old nephew and his boyfriend, and the boyfriend's two-year-old son), a job during the day earning worthless pesos (I was a security guard at the Museum of Fine Arts), and a job at night earning hard currency (I washed dishes at a fancy family-run restaurant, a position I got by marrying—that's right, *marrying*—the owner because Cuban law demands that family businesses only hire family). My Havana was dirty and teeming, and so loud it sometimes felt like a piercing in my ears. I honestly could not remember the last time I'd been alone for more than it takes to relieve myself, and even then I wasn't immune to the soundtrack of screaming and clattering.

Given my age—thirty-four—and my situation, I'd already been with pretty much everybody I was going to be with in Havana. And given how overcrowded we were at home (I slept in the same sweat-drenched bed with my nephew, his boyfriend, and their two-year-old, or, weather permitting, on a hammock I'd strung up that ran parallel with the clothesline in the tenement's back patio), I knew nobody was going to move in with me, even if she loved me, and I wasn't sure I brought enough to the table, in spite of my dollar-earning dishwashing job, to be wanted enough to take home. In the few instances when the possibility arose, it was only because the other girl's overcrowded home mirrored mine, but with an additional half-dozen cousins from the provinces. That only left tourists as romantic possibilities, and though my English is fine, nothing calmed my ardor quicker than some American telling me all about the wonders of the Revolution as she paid my way into a dollars-only club I would otherwise not be able to afford.

In fact, I was celebrating the visa my father had gotten me at precisely one of those clubs, listening to a pretty terrible reggaeton band whose terribleness was underscored by a terrible sound system, when I experienced the tumor's first overt symptom. In an instant, the bass just dropped out of the music.

It became tinny and thin. Because the sound quality at all Havana venues—even the very best ones—is unpredictable, I was sure it had nothing to do with me. I was with a bunch of friends, typical Cubans, and a Canadian who was being hustled by one of those friends and had paid for all of us. I shrugged an apology her way and she smiled uncertainly in my direction.

When we left a few hours later, my left ear felt plugged. A loud argument was taking place as we passed a café and a drunk blared a trumpet at the corner, but it all sounded gauzy and far away.

Oh, I know that feeling: my ears got waterlogged when I went diving in the Maldives, the Canadian said.

Everybody nodded as if they knew the exact coordinates of the Maldives, afraid to seem ignorant in front of the Canadian, but I wondered if it wasn't one of those countries where Cuba had sent medical brigades. I was pretty sure I'd seen something in a documentary; Cuban TV is one long parade of documentaries. In any case, I hadn't been diving, ever, in my whole life, but I did wonder, immediately, if going deep underwater meant peace and solitude or if all those schools of fish and shivers of sharks made you feel just as crowded as the city and maybe even a little paranoid.

Do you have hydrogen peroxide at home? the Canadian asked. Pour some in your ear—it'll sound like fireworks—then lie on your side and it'll clear up.

But it didn't, and I suspect it wouldn't have even if we'd had hydrogen peroxide. In fact, over the next few days my hearing seemed to fluctuate wildly. Most of the time, it felt like everything was at a great distance, as if everyone were talking to me from the bottom of the sea. My mother told me she thought it was stress, and that seemed a reasonable explanation. After all, I was leaving soon, headed to the great unknown of the United States, and though I wasn't planning on living with my father, legally I did have to stay with him for a year and a day because he was sponsoring me. I hadn't seen him in more than a decade; I hadn't heard his voice in almost that long when he'd called out of the blue to say he wanted to save me. My mother said it must all be happening for a reason.

My hearing got no better as I prepped for my trip, but by the time I was ready to go, I must have gotten used to it because I wasn't paying attention to it anymore. Then, as I was getting on the plane, waving at my family waving at me from the tarmac— my grandmother's boyfriend has a relative who's a high-ranking airport official so they all got to personally escort me to the plane—I felt a twitching in my left eye. I'd been very sad, especially as I waved at my grandmother wondering if I'd ever see her again, but I hadn't been able to cry, or, more precisely, to cry in any kind of recognizable fashion. My right eye teared but my left remained stoic. And now this: little electrical flashes flaring across my eyeball. Because, you see, it was *in* my eyeball—not on my eyelid, not on my brow—but right there, *in* my eye, as if my retina had developed a tic. For a few minutes, I saw double and I had difficulty climbing the airplane stairs and finding my seat. Everyone assumed I was just too emotional to make sense of boarding.

But the twitching didn't go away. At customs in Miami, it got so bad I was actually asked by an agent if I needed medical attention. I said I didn't, that I was just nervous about my new life, which my trembling hands seemed to authenticate. What had me genuinely concerned was that my left eye now felt as if someone was constantly opening and shutting a set of blinds. I was supposed to have two hours of rest before I caught my next flight to San Francisco, but assuming it was the prospect of seeing my father that had triggered my state, I quickly pulled out my contact list—the list every Cuban has of who they'll call if they ever get off the island—and asked a passenger from my flight if I could borrow her cell phone. I tried to calm down enough to dial.

One of the advantages of my worthless museum

security guard job was that I got to meet a lot of foreigners, especially artists. They were usually busy proving their proletariat bona fides to the other Cubans—who never talked to us—by making nice with guards and janitors and such. That's how I'd gotten to know a video artist named Laura Vaas when she had a one-woman show at the museum. During her installation, it'd frequently been just her and me through many an afternoon, and I'd proven a good helper and sounding board. Before she left Cuba, she'd given me her number and said to call her if I ever found myself in Miami.

This is who again? Laura asked after I'd identified myself. The volume was up high enough that the phone's owner heard her and looked at me with concern.

I told her my name again. From the museum in Havana, I said.

To my surprise, Laura didn't hesitate once I explained about my father the avenging Christian and the way my body had gone into revolt at the thought of seeing him. In about an hour she was exactly where she said she'd be, at a Starbucks in Terminal D East just outside the security check. I've never been so relieved in my life; I honestly don't know what I would have done if she hadn't shown up. The twitch in my eye went into overdrive while I waited.

Laura greeted me with a hug that far exceeded our island acquaintance, grabbed my single suitcase, and drove me to her home, which turned out to be not a palace on the beach but a small wooden house in Kendall with a garage that served as her studio. I almost asked her what had happened, that I thought she was a successful artist, but I caught myself: she was driving a 2002 Ford Focus Wagon. By Cuban standards that's practically a luxury car, but I knew, even in the airport parking lot where it was surrounded by scores of newer, shinier cars, that I'd probably misjudged her situation.

That very night, after settling me into her guest bedroom, Laura gave me a spare laptop—a *spare* laptop!—and set up an account for me on Facebook. She suggested I try to find people I knew in the States. I told her about my contact list but she said on Facebook all you needed was somebody's name, that I didn't need their phone number or address. I sat at the kitchen table long after she went to bed, one hand covering my jittery eye, the other typing in name after name of people I knew from Cuba who'd been long gone.

I was on an old friend's page when I saw some pictures of myself from the very night my ear had started giving me trouble. There I was dancing, though you could see from my expression something was wrong. Then I noticed the Canadian was also in one of the frames. My friend had tagged her and I followed the link to her page where I discovered there was a whole album—132 pictures—of her trip to Cuba, including many places I'd never even heard of, like a beach called María la Gorda in an area that had been declared a Biosphere Reserve by UNESCO. This was a Cuba unknown to me: all parrot fish and blurry hummingbirds, with only the occasional brown arm helping the Canadian onto a boat or serving her and her friends a bountiful meal.

I scanned her other albums and saw she was quite the world traveler: swimming with green sea turtles in the Philippines, with moray eels in the Solomon Islands, and walking along what appeared to be a beach at night with blue-white stars scattered in the sand, as if the sky had emptied a constellation on the shore. I wondered if my eye was playing tricks on me. The caption read: *Ostracod crustaceans, kind of like bioluminescent phytoplankton, lighting up the shore in Mudhdhoo Island in the Maldives*. I thought: Wow.

I stayed up close to dawn searching for more photos of this strange phenomenon but mostly finding image after image of beaches and beach towns in the Maldives: little storybook villages with an infinite span of blue-green water surrounding them, the sky an endless and tender light. Nothing looked crowded in the Maldives, and even in the capital city of Male, houses were wreathed by gardens of blue and orange flowers, hammocks everywhere. Best of all, of the approximately 1,200 islands that make up the country—and I say approximately because the number of islands depends on the season—only about two hundred are inhabited, and only half of those have tourist resorts. Honestly, I couldn't figure out why UNESCO hadn't declared all of the Maldives a Biosphere Reserve.

The next day, I opened my eyes and everything was in perfect focus: the ceiling fan above Laura's guest bed, the floral print on the duvet, the giant black screen on the wall with its blinking red light. It took me a second to remember where I was—the United States, Miami, the home of someone I barely knew—and then I heard a low bass throbbing through the wall and the sharp knock of Laura's knuckles on the bedroom door.

Adelante, I said, and in she came with a tray holding a glass of orange juice, a banana, a stack of pancakes, and a small cup of black coffee with a full head of foam.

You won't get service like this every day, she said, but today being your first day in America . . .

I almost said something about America being the entirety of the Western Hemisphere but gratitude shut me up. Instead I asked her how to make the picture of the glow-in-the-dark beach in the Maldives the wallpaper on my new laptop.

In truth, Laura Vaas turned out to be an exceptional friend. When I further explained my situation—including that I wouldn't have a green card or a work permit for a year and a day—she got on the phone and found me a job washing dishes at a restaurant owned by some friends of hers who paid me in cash. She also got me odd jobs with other artists packing work for shipping. I wasn't making a ton of money, but enough to buy a bus pass, go to a movie now and again, and buy groceries and creams for my chapped hands. Then Laura said she was going on a fellowship to London for part of the year and would have had to pay someone to house-sit if I hadn't shown up. My free housing would continue, so even though I was sending money to my family every month, I was even able to start saving.

I did get a cell phone pretty quickly, and I did eventually call my father and thank him for getting me out of Cuba. He was furious with me, accused me of using him just to come over, but I made no effort to explain how I'd gotten sick just thinking about living with him. Part of it was that as time had passed and my vision and hearing returned to normal, it was hard to believe my symptoms hadn't been psychosomatic, and I just didn't want to give him that kind of power.

In spite of having my new cell, I didn't make other calls. I knew people in Miami and Key West and Tampa, but I actually didn't want to see anyone. I folded up my contact list and put it away. Laura's house was blissfully quiet—all I ever heard were little warblers up in the palm trees and the mailman lifting the letter slot in the afternoon. My bed, which Laura constantly apologized for because it was only a single, felt as long and wide as a luxury liner to me.

Initially, I had tried to pay Laura back for her kindness by cooking and cleaning, but she got upset, said she was gaining weight, that she liked to take care of her stuff herself. I was terrified I'd offended her so I just tried to stay out of her way and holed up in the guest room. I watched a lot of TV on the big screen in my room, especially documentaries, including *The Island President*, about how the Maldives are disappearing due to rising sea levels caused by climate change. The Maldivian president wants the world to learn a lesson from his country's predicament. He wants the world to take responsibility. The situation is so bad they've even got a sovereign-land fund to buy new territory and move once their country's submerged, like Alexandria and the pyramids of Yonaguni in Japan. Or like Guanacabibes, an underwater city off Cuba's western shore, except no one who isn't Cuban actually thinks it's a city, just a bunch of geological anomalies.

As soon as Laura left for London, I ended my self-imposed exile in the guest room. I opened every door in the house and danced from room to room. What splendor to open my arms wide and just feel cool, satiny air-conditioning on my skin. What extravagance to take a hot forty-minute shower in the morning and a cool hour-long bath at night. I walked around naked and whistled and even did cartwheels in the living room.

I thought for sure I'd grow lonesome at some point but I didn't. I got plenty of human interaction at the restaurant and on the bus. Every now and again I'd run into someone I knew, and when I evaded their questions they assumed I was either having a mysterious affair with a rich American or spying for Cuba. They'd write my mother and then she'd write me and we'd both laugh about it.

One night at the restaurant, I was loading the dishwasher and singing along to a new song by Calle 13 when somebody turned off the radio. Hey, I said, c'mon, as I reached for a pair of latex gloves to tackle the pots. But the music didn't come back on. I walked over to the radio and turned up the dial and almost immediately one of the owners swatted my hand away. He was saying something—his mouth was moving and his face showed irritation—but I couldn't hear a thing. I shook my head but the bubble tightened: suddenly I could only see him through what appeared to be a fish-eye lens. He grabbed me by the shoulders and brought his face close to mine, but I couldn't understand him.

Before I knew it, the other owner, a Panamanian guy who had been trying to set me up with his fifty-two-year-old sister, threw me in his Jeep and drove me to the emergency room at Jackson Memorial Hospital. We were there until dawn and he stayed with me the whole time, occasionally squeezing my hand and bringing me something to eat or drink. The ER wasn't much different than Ciro García in Havana, except that the electricity didn't go out the whole time we were there. Otherwise, it was the same defeated faces, the same resignation to whatever fate had just been ordained by a fall or accident or, in my case, a sudden short-circuit.

They found the tumor when they did an MRI of my brain. It sat dead center in my skull, shaped like a two-inch comma and leaning heavily to the left. It had wrapped itself around my auditory nerve so as to practically strangle it. It was also big enough to damage both cranial nerves four and five, which explained why I'd had double vision and wasn't able to tear up. What they couldn't tell me was why I had hearing loss in both ears. They needed to run more tests. Unless I did something, they said via notes the Panamanian wrote out in his boxy script, both my hearing and vision would slowly deteriorate. They talked about surgery and radiation, experimental medicines and treatments like the cyber knife and auditory brain implants, all of which I could never afford. The restaurant didn't offer health insurance and I wouldn't have been eligible anyway, since I had to wait a year and a day before I could get my US residence and work permit. I wouldn't die from this tumor, they told me, but left alone it would eventually leave me trapped in my own body.

After the Panamanian took me home, I sat in Laura's expansive living room and thought about my predicament. My father would tell me this was a punishment from God for all my sins, for all the women I'd briefly loved. My mother would tell me it was destiny, that there are forces in the universe greater than us that we simply must obey. Was there anything to learn, for anyone, from my situation? Who would take responsibility for me?

I got myself a beer from Laura's fridge and counted my money. I had saved about eight thousand dollars. I was considering buying a ticket back to Havana, knowing that with that money my family could probably take care of me for a very long time. I had no illusions about my condition being relieved in Havana. Certainly, I would get medical attention, I would be visited by doctors. But I knew Cuba simply didn't have the equipment or expertise to help me. And I didn't want to have brain surgery at a hospital where the power went off and on without regard to what was happening on the operating table.

I opened my laptop to send an e-mail to an acquaintance from the museum who had agreed to relay messages to my mother in case of emergency. When I saw my wallpaper, that blue-white constellation across the coastline in the Maldives, I knew time was of the essence. I might not ever hear the waves lapping the shore, but my vision, at least at that moment, was again as good as a high-power Leica lens. When I searched for one-way tickets to Male, I found they were within my reach.

In the weeks following my arrival, I got a job washing dishes. I figure I can do that, or maybe gardening, until my eyes fail. Then I will sail to one of those islands where no one goes and lay myself down in all that phosphorescence. I will sink into the firmament of the Maldives one centimeter at a time and let the waters rise, lifting me, guiding me through the silent dark to my own Atlantis.

# THE TOWER OF THE ANTILLES

*with thanks to Kcho,*
*for Archipiélago en mi pensamiento*

## 1.

What is your name?

You already know my name.

What is your name?

You already know my name.

They went on like this, one with his line, the other with hers.

What . . .

You already know . . .

. . .

They coincided, not exactly in harmony: one voice was a little reedy, though steady, the other flat.

The room was black and moist. Things may have been slithering about, small harmless things. The faint cataphonics of carpentry whispered from the solitary window.

What is your name?

This time, silence.

What is your name?

His chair bumped along on the sandy floor. When he stretched, his body distracted the lightest breeze from her face. The wooden beat from outside continued, still dim.

A door opened, shut. In between, a vague rustle.

### 2.

In truth, there's only speculation about the formation of the island, carved by lava and tides, how the tips of peaks became mountains, and islet after islet merged, thousands of them, until they became an archipelago shaped like a curved cicatrix.

The island's natives did not know how to cultivate land or use tools. They picked fruit, chased crabs out of their sandy wells. They grew root vegetables, usually in mounds of soil designed to retard erosion and lengthen storage, and knew how to make bread from an otherwise poisonous tuber. They fished, hunted rats and iguanas, and ate both turtles and dogs.

The men went naked for the most part, the women frequently wore short skirts but breasts were generally bared. They flattened their foreheads by binding them with a hard plate before they were fully formed. This way their heads slanted, reflecting light back to the heavens.

They were terrible, unambitious mariners, with

no sense at all for navigation. For a while, in fact, many believed the island was no island at all, but a monstrous raft made of packed dirt and clay, impossible to pilot.

They had two supreme gods, each with a particular allegiance to water: a lord of the sea and a goddess of rivers and abundance. These accepted prayer and platefuls of food as reverence: plump marlin filets, papayas bursting with pockets of gooey black seeds, buckets of coconut milk.

Before making offerings, devotees had to cleanse themselves through absolution, fasting, and ritualized vomiting. Hungrily, they put wooden spades down their throats, liturgical implements they lazily let slide from their lips.

Afterward, they used a long, straw-like tube to sniff the pulverized bark of a local tree, which caused extreme hallucinations.

### 3.

What is your name? he asked.

Pinewood is best, easy to whittle, she thought to herself. The island was dense with mahogany, cedar, and palm trees with feathery leaf bouquets.

You already know my name, she said through lips that were a little sore.

She coughed. She knew even then how important

it was to choose wood without knots, blemishes, or cracks. She thought of nothing but the pulpy inner flesh of trees, of Madras muslin and hemp.

What is your name?

Her boat needed a brace. About five centimeters thick, a meter wide, and two and a quarter meters long. In her head, she measured roughly thirty centimeters from one edge toward the center. She marked the points, then drew diagonal lines across it.

What is your name?

She continued counting off intimate distances, her fingers designing on the tender canvas of her thighs.

### 4.

One day, a very large brown woman with slanted eyes set a tiny boat on the island's shore. It was made from the languid leaves of a local flower, folded over this way and that until the triangle in the middle signaled completion. Only a few of the natives noticed, or cared, and when the tiny boat was found missing among the usual debris at dawn, everyone presumed the tide's eager tendrils were to blame.

That afternoon, the large brown woman with slanted eyes returned, this time with a boat of balsa wood. Its skin was as smooth as a baby's, pink and sweet. Again, it vanished overnight.

During that week, boats began to appear—canoes

and kayaks, floats made of driftwood, hollowed tree trunks, discarded refrigerators made buoyant with inflated tubes, car chassis with water wings. They piled one on top of the other, each seeming to decrease in size as the structure ascended, so that they began to form separate stories. Each level had its own peculiar color, usually a variation of white-washed blue, or a smear of dense aquamarine.

Later, the boats began to pivot, a little each, so that soon there were prows of a sort directed to the four points of the compass. There was nothing between the vessels, each one perfectly balanced on top of the other, so that they swayed with the trade winds, waved to the waters, but did not fall.

### 5.

Eventually, he stopped asking her name. He would just come in and sit across from her for a while in the darkness. She'd grown accustomed to the visits. Her thighs were covered with ghostly designs for boats. After a time, he'd scrape the chair backward, get up, and disappear.

Then her lips would soundlessly form the words that followed him: *You already know my name.*

### 6.

On the island's coast, a few mangy dogs, bats, and

a tempest or two of wild bees came to rest on the column of boats. It swelled with frogs in its crevices, snails crawled the walls. Birds with feathers frazzled like uncombed hair perched and called. There were clear days and days of fog, nights when the stars flashed across the sky and others when they refused to shine.

That was usually when the boats would moan from the weight of the natives scaling the tower.

## Acknowledgments

My gratitude always to María Eugenia Alegría, Kalisha Buckhannon, Adrián Castro, Natalie Catasús, David Driscoll, Sarah Frank, Elise Johnson, Michelle Kirchner, Kim McGowan, Bayo Ojikutu, Patrick Reichard, Jane Saks, Humberto Sánchez, and Jasmine Wade.

Carolina de Robertis, a very wonderful writer and friend, generously read and edited this collection for me. Everything has benefited from her fine touch.

Cecilia Vaisman read a number of these stories, but she also missed a few. I'm thankful for the many years of encouragement and praise, for the words every artist needs to hear that she so generously offered. I wish I could have seen her face, heard her reactions, to the new stories. I wish we were at her kitchen table, in Chicago or Havana, talking about so many things. I miss her all the time, every single day.

No one, of course, has been more important to this project, and to all of my projects, than Megan Bayles. I'd be so adrift without her. A nod, too, to Ilan Bayles Obejas, because he's the reason for everything now.

I'm forever grateful to USA Artists for my 2014 Ford Foundation Fellowship, which made my life one hundred times easier and helped me complete this book.

Lastly, and always, I'm in awe of Akashic's beautiful and soulful team: Johnny, Johanna, Ibrahim, Aaron, Susannah, and the rest.

"The Cola of Oblivion" was first published in *The Butter*, edited by Roxane Gay, which was part of *The Toast*, March 2015.

"Kimberle" appeared in *ACM 50: The Chicago Issue*, edited by Jacob Knabb, December 2010; and in *Ambientes: New Queer Latino Writing*, edited by Lázaro Lima and Felice Picano, June 2011; in the original Spanish, it was included in *Aguas y Otros Cuentos*, published by Letras Cubanas in Cuba, July 2009; and in *Cuentos*, Literal Publishing, 2017.

"The Maldives" was first published in *Prairie Schooner*, Vol. 90, No. 1, Spring 2016.

"The Tower of the Antilles" appeared in the *Cincinnati Romance Review*, Vol. 40, Spring 2016; and in *Otium*, Vol. 2, No. 4, January 2006.

"Waters" was first published in *The Vintage Book of International Lesbian Fiction*, edited by Naomi Holoch and Joan Nestle, June 1999.